~ SUMMER OF FIFTY-SEVEN ~

～SUMMER OF FIFTY-SEVEN～

Coming of Age
in
Wyoming's Shining Mountains

STEPHEN C. JOSEPH

SUNSTONE
PRESS

SANTA FE

Photograph of the Cessna 172 on the cover
appears courtesy of Cessna Aircraft Company.

Sunstone books may be purchased for educational, business, or sales promotional
use. For information please write: Special Markets Department, Sunstone Press,
P.O. Box 2321, Santa Fe, New Mexico 87504-2321.

Library of Congress Cataloging-in-Publication Data:
Joseph, Stephen C.
    Summer of fifty-seven: coming of age in Wyoming's shining mountains / Stephen
C. Joseph.—1st ed.
        p. cm.
    ISBN: 0-86534-367-5 (hardcover)   ISBN: 0-86534-473-6 (softcover)
        1. Mountain life—Fiction. 2. Young men—Fiction. 3. Wyoming—Fiction.
I. Title: Summer of '57. II. Title.

PS3610.O676 S86 2002
813'.6—dc21   2002030200

WWW.SUNSTONEPRESS.COM
SUNSTONE PRESS / POST OFFICE BOX 2321 / SANTA FE, NM 87504-2321 /USA
(505) 988-4418 / *ORDERS ONLY* (800) 243-5644 / FAX (505) 988-1025

— For Jedediah Strong Smith, who opened the way,

And for Elliot and Jason Martin, who will find their own.

For a boy's will is the wind's will,
And the thoughts of youth are long, long thoughts.

—Henry Wadworth Longfellow, 1807–1882

He who has not a good memory
Should never take upon himself
The trade of lying.

—Michel de Montaigne, 1533–1592

JACKSON HOLE AND WYOMING'S SHINING MOUNTAINS

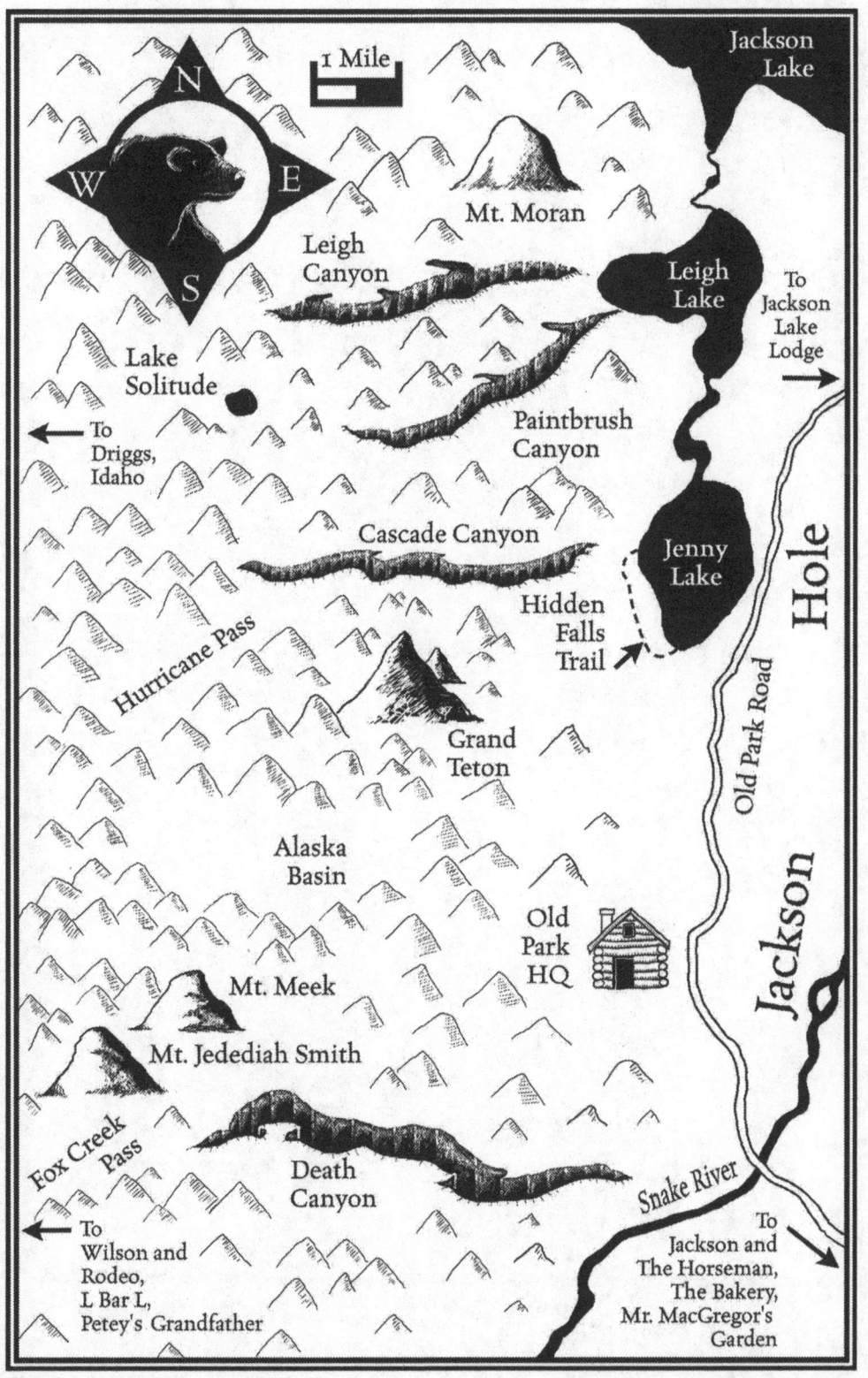

⟶ FOREWORD ⟶

Our tendency to paste headline labels upon decades (such as "The Fifties: The Silent Generation") is misleading for at least two reasons. First, any ten-year period in American history is suffused with such variety, across all facets of life, that any single label is of necessity simplistic. But, second, carving off ten-year periods that start out with a year whose terminal numeral is zero, and end with a year possessing the terminal numeral nine, places artificial and rather irrelevant bookends in the river of time, inevitably adrift, bobbing askew in the currents.

One could argue that the crux that was to shape American culture for the remainder of the Twentieth Century, that was of primary impact in shifting virtually all the ground from "before" to "after", took place during the latter years of the Fifties and the early years of the Sixties.

From: Eisenhower Two, the coming of Castro, Jim Crow at Little Rock, the Bomb, the emergence of television as a major entertainment and commercial force, Sputnik, Elvis and the bridging of the black/white divide in popular music.

To: John Kennedy alive and then assassinated, the Beatles, the Bay of Pigs, the Pill, videotape and the primacy of television as the primary information source, Martin Luther King.

If there was ever a time "before the deluge," it was that crux. At the beginning, there was a prevalent adhesion to Mom and Apple Pie, within a generally accepted cultural and social order. By the end, there were Vietnam and the Rebellions of '68, and everything was up for grabs.

Red Skelton, a brilliant mime and comedian of those decades, performed a TV skit that exemplifies well that late-Fifties/early-Sixties crux:

The drunkard's wife decides, once and for all, to teach him a lesson. She inverts the furniture and objects of his living room, nailing the furniture to the ceiling, on which is glued the carpet, hanging the pictures and mirrors upside down, and so forth.

Skelton enters after a night on the town, unsteady of gait, humming tunelessly to himself, smiling innocently. He stops, confused. Everything is familiar. Everything is, in one sense, in its proper place. And yet nothing obeys the laws of memory or the laws of accepted physics. He, himself, is marooned on the ceiling, and unable to get himself "right side up." Lost in space.

To have come of age in the late 1950's, as a White American Male, was to have your fingers upon the door handle of that room, but to have not as yet turned the knob.

This is one story, of such a time, and place, and person.

~ PREFACE ~

This is a work of imagination. It is also a work of experience. There is truth in the old saw that all fiction has significant autobiographical elements. There is also truth in the statement that all autobiography contains significant fictions. Thus, in this book, the conventional disclaimer about "resemblance to any persons living or dead" loses meaningful relevance.

There are many people whom I wish to thank. Jim Smith of Sunstone Press became a partner in this effort. Kent Carroll was extremely generous with advice and encouragement, when advice was plentiful, but encouragement very hard to come by. I am blessed that my wife, Beth Preble, is not only my muse, but also my clearest-eyed critic. My daughter and son-in-law, Denise and Peter Joseph-Martin, produced my wild buckaroo grandsons who are the proximate stimulus to putting this four-decades-old dream down on paper. The music of Woody Guthrie burned into my younger memory the relationship of song to story, and I thank the Woody Guthrie Foundation for keeping the song going. My best buddy, Typhoon, curled as a pup at my feet when I wrote my previous book. She performed the same service now again, in her twilight years.

And finally, I would like to thank the men and women of the US National Park Service and the US Forest Service, past, present, and future, for their dedication to conserving our most irreplaceable treasures.

Santa Fe, New Mexico
2002

⸺ ACKNOWLEDGEMENTS ⸺

Dust Bowl Refugee
Words and Music by Woody Guthrie
TRO-copyright 1960 (renewed),1963 (renewed) Ludlow Music, Inc.
New York, NY ⸺ used by permission

Going Down the Road
(I Ain't Going to Be Treated This Way)
Words and Music by Woody Guthrie and Lee Hays
TRO-copyright 1960 (renewed),1963 (renewed) Ludlow Music, Inc.
New York, NY ⸺ used by permission

Pastures of Plenty
Words and Music by Woody Guthrie
TRO-copyright 1960 (renewed), 1963 (renewed) Ludlow Music, Inc.
New York, NY ⸺ used by permission

900 Miles
Words and Music by Woody Guthrie
Copyright 1958 (renewed) by SANGA Music, Inc.
All rights reserved ⸺ used by permission

— From Boston to Moose Junction —

It was merely a few months past my nineteenth birthday, during the late winter of 1956-1957, when I decided to ride my thumb to Alaska, four thousand miles and more.

Who knows how, or where, such desires take root, from what long-hidden seeds they sprout. Are they stirred in from the genetic soup of grandparents who left the Old World for the New? Are they remembered from whispered words of stories or lullabies heard near the dawn of life? Are they lessons learned in school and at the movies, of Boone and Crockett, of Huck Finn, and, later, of Shane?

I have a scratchy eight millimeter old home movie film: the family at a picnic in the woods of the lower Hudson Valley. All, except one, are gathered around the wooden table. Then, out from among the trees, knobby knees striding under short pants, a crude walking stick waving, comes three-year-old me, unmistakable joy on my face and in my heart. If I had been old enough, I undoubtedly would have been whistling. Could I have known then that the archetypal American myth is that of the lone wanderer, the one who rides in and then rides on, looking always only for the next mountain, and again and again pushed over the hill and far away by the sight of a neighbor's chimney smoke? Call me Ishmael?

Later, in early adolescence, it was Western dime novels (though they indeed cost twenty-five, and sometimes thirty-five cents even in those long-ago days). In compulsive ritual, every Friday after school I would pedal my bike the three miles to a favored cigar store, spend what seemed like hours choosing from among the books on the racks, and pedal home again. What fantasies galloped along with that two-wheeled and many-spoked magic steed, pushing across the suburban prairie, carrying the precious mail by Pony Express! Once home, I would read the week's treasure as slowly as possible, making it last, obsessively, until the next Friday. With Max Brand, Evan Evans, Peter Field, Luke Short, and a score of other authors, I stole horses from around Kiowa campfires, drove long-horned, half-wild cattle across the Cimarron, rescued the widow's ranch from the banker who wore the black string tie, held out against all odds at Fort Apache, and most, most of all, lived as a Free Trapper in the 1830s Shining Mountains.

With the zany compulsiveness of adolescence, I held my treasures in a special, separate bookcase, arranged alphabetically by author, nested within unique sections by publisher: Pocket Books, Signet Books, Bantam Books, and the new, 'expensive' Ballantines. Dreams were filled with the contents of that bookcase. The Black Hills, the Arizona Territory, Texas to Wyoming, the endless grass of Montana, and, striding north to south across my paradise, what we call the Rockies, and what the earliest white men who saw them called the Shining Mountains. At school, I drew maps, both accurate and fictional ones, of that country of the heart, hiding my work behind a bent head close to a propped-up schoolbook. I memorized the illustrations in the *Encyclopedia Britannica* that chronicled the westward march of Manifest Destiny.

I roamed, with my Daisy Red Ryder Carbine BB-gun, the shrinking woods and weeded lots of my suburban town, shooting (I blush to say) robins and squirrels, seeing in my mind's eye the tall grass prairie and the bison, the mountain forests and the elk. By twelve or thirteen, I had prevailed upon my father to purchase for me three antiques: a 45 caliber

Sharps buffalo gun, an 1874 Springfield military carbine, and an old Stevens pump 22. All were non-functional, at least to everyone but me. They rested in a rack on my bedroom wall, and every night, just before sleep, I would take them down one by one, check that they were cleaned and oiled (they always were), and aim them at the invisible targets of my imagination: loaded, cocked, sighted-in, and trigger-pulled.

In my nineteenth year I was a sophomore at an excellent college: a "grind" pre-med in a decade when the one phrase defined the other. I was a pretty good, and very aggressive, athlete, an A-student with little fundamental comprehension of the relevance and significance of what I was learning, and, not by choice, a virgin (my knowledge of detailed female anatomy and physiology mostly gleaned from what was then known as "heavy petting" and, upon rare occasions, reciprocal digital stimulation).

Most importantly, I felt the world closing in upon me, rather than opening out before me. I could see a clear road ahead, but narrowing, narrowing. As has perhaps been true forever for young males who don't quite feel that they fit, I yearned to break free, to measure myself by my own, rather than others', benchmarks, to seek a frontier not yet closed.

I spent hours haunting the library of the Anthropology Department, voraciously reading the accounts of the early students of the Plains Indians, of the Northwest Coast, of the Arctic peoples. And then, one wet, cold Boston March afternoon, I came upon a hand-written 3x5 file card tacked to the library bulletin board:

"Wanted: Riders to share expenses and driving to California.
Leave early June. Call Gene at 824-9787."

So, perhaps, riding with Gene part-way to California wouldn't exactly be crossing the Cumberland Gap with Boone, but it could be a first leg to Alaska.

Alaska seemed to me to be what was left of all I had dreamed of. It was expected that Alaskan statehood would take place in either 1958 or 1959, truly closing the American frontier. If I could get there before that fact, while it was still the Alaska Territory, I could have a taste of what my heroes had felt in the Dakota Territory, in Montana in the early days, in Arizona and New Mexico before 1912. If not, it might be all gone, forever, and something might also go out of my young life with it, something I would never know, but always regret the absence of.

And so, in the second week of June, Gene, Allan, and I piled into a creaky Chevy, and pulled out of Cambridge, headed, as the best dreams on this continent have always been directed, West. My plan was to ride the Lincoln Highway with them as far as Rock Springs, Wyoming, there to leave them and then strike out alone north through Yellowstone to Montana, and up across the Canadian border to the Alaskan Highway. That road was scarcely 15 years old, four years younger than myself, pushed through the muskeg and mountains as the AlCan Highway by military engineers, to forge a land route from the Lower 48 to Alaska, and thus to pre-empt a possible Japanese invasion through the Aleutian Islands. The Road West, and the Road North, were fused in my mind.

Family and friends were aghast. But knowing my stubbornness and eccentricities, no one raised much of a fuss; my folks kissed me good-bye over the phone, and my friends just shook their heads.

After much thought, and some experimentation, here is what I took with me. On my back (below a 1950s 'crew-cut' so short as to preclude the need for repetition by a licensed barber for some time to come): a short denim Wrangler jacket, the one with the metal buttons, washed soft and supple. A cotton work shirt. A nondescript Bulova watch with leather band. Denim jeans (we called them "dungarees" or "Levi's" then, and you never, ever, turned up the cuffs unless you were a girl, or a city guy). Cotton 'sweat socks', and a pair of poorly broken-in Red Wing work boots.

A broad plain leather belt, from which hung a four-inch leather case enclosing a bone-handled pocket knife with four blades: long and short cutting, a slot screwdriver/bottle-opener, and an awl. No hat, no sunglasses, both of which were then considered to be affectations.

In my hand: a weathered Gladstone bag, the kind that opens from a top zipper to offer broad and square access. Inside the bag: three extra shirts (one a warm flannel), three 'T-shirts', all the same plain white (no funny illustrations or double-entendre slogans, no designer logos in those days), three pairs of Jockey shorts (the fourth I wore under my Levi's), the other three pairs of sweat socks, two extra handkerchiefs and a red-checked bandanna, a spare pair of Levi's, a pair of white Converse 'Hi-Top' sneakers, a shaving kit (toothbrush and paste, a Gillette 'safety' razor and packet of individually-wrapped double-edged 'Blueblades', a small plastic soap case for washing and shaving, a travel shaving brush, a small metal mirror, and a few Band-Aids), a hand towel, a half-roll of toilet paper crushed flat, wooden kitchen 'Strike Anywhere' matches and a small candle, a small flashlight with the old grey, blue, and red 'Every Ready' batteries, and a hundred feet of parachute cord.

Strapped to the top of the Gladstone, between its handles: a light cotton sleeping bag, protectively wrapped inside a rubberized Army surplus rain poncho.

In my pockets: no keys at all—surely the sign of the liberated road traveler. A wallet with my identification (including my draft card), pictures of my mom and dad, brother, and dog, and a rolled-up condom. The latter had rested hopefully, but unsuccessfully, in the wallet for so long it had created a permanent circled ridge in the leather; Planned Parenthood should be grateful that I, like many American boys, never got the chance to use that particular dried and aged device. But I was ever hopeful, and, as the Tom Lehrer song of that era advised, was prepared to "Be Prepared." I had about one hundred and twenty dollars, some in my wallet, some in the Gladstone, and the majority tucked in a plastic bag under the sole of my left foot in the Red Wing boots.

Gene and Allan were neither scintillating nor sympathetic companions, being graduate students at the Business School, and thus intolerant of both my callowness and my adventuresome idealism. But I was a full-share paying passenger, didn't fill the Chevy with heavy luggage, and thus was, in their view, a reasonable cost/benefit addition. We didn't talk much, the radio filling the silence with Chubby Checkers, Fats Domino, and The King. The miles rolled by: Boston down through old Routes 16 and 30 to Connecticut and the Wilbur Cross Parkway, through Hartford where the gas wars always allowed you to fill up at an economical thirty-two cents per gallon, into the New York suburbs and across the George Washington bridge, struggling down the Jersey Turnpike until we reached the old Pennsy Turnpike, one of the country's earliest-built, controlled-access, long-distance roads.

Somewhere in western Pennsylvania, we stopped for the first night. Gene and Allan looked for a motel in the farm town along the pike, but I was counting dollars for the miles ahead, and determined to lie up in the woods, where they would retrieve me the following morning. I rolled my bag out in a low and sheltered spot as dusk approached, lulled by the sound of a distant tractor, using the last of the Daylight Savings Time light to cultivate a few more rows. Soon the closer-in whine of mosquitoes drowned out the tractor, and I was faced with an uncomfortable choice, one that would often recur that summer. You either put the rubberized poncho over your face, neck, and hands, and sweltered, or hunched over as close as you could at the top of the short bag, and bled. Alaska seemed very far away, and I felt very small and alone.

Somehow, dawn arrived, my companions of the road re-appeared, and we moved on, through Ohio, Indiana, Illinois, to Iowa, along Route 30, the old Lincoln Highway, which would take me all the way to Rock Springs in western Wyoming. Green country, endless rows of corn just coming up to ankle height, squared-off dirt section roads enclosing farmland, and that corn stretching to the ever-receding horizon. The Lincoln Highway was mostly two-lane, sometimes three-lane, blacktop, and you had to be careful, going fifty-five miles an hour or more, watching for farm tractors turning out of the section roads onto the Way West.

Crossing the Mississippi River meant little to me, but the thought of crossing the Missouri, the route of Lewis and Clark and of the fur-trading keelboat men, the route to the Big Sky country, stirred my blood.

We had stopped for the night in the college town of Ames, Iowa, where the world-weary proprietress of a homey motel looked doubtfully at the three of us when Gene asked for a "double room." Accepting my pleas to be allowed to sleep on the floor in my bag between the two beds, and possibly touched by the sight of the swollen lumps on my face, she agreed to charge only my companions. I dined upon what I believe was my third burger and malt of the trip, and got a good night's rest on the hard floor.

The third day saw another endless haul, this time across Nebraska and Wyoming. On the outskirts of a small Nebraska town, I saw a posted sign that has puzzled me to this day: 'Swedes—we don't want your kind here. Move on.' It was not the bigotry, but the unusual choice of ethnicity, that I have not been able to comprehend.

Southern Wyoming was mostly dry and broken country, marked at long intervals during the last century where the head of track of railroad construction had left a good-sized town. And each town, in descending pecking order from east to west, had been graced with a public institution: Cheyenne (State Capitol), Laramie (State University), Rawlins (State Prison), and Evanston (State Mental Hospital).

In the mid-afternoon, we arrived in Rock Springs, a dusty grey straggling place that certainly looked to me to be at least seven parts rock to less than one part springs. Gene, Allan, and I grunted our good-byes, I stepped out of the Chevrolet, hauled out my Gladstone, and stood on the north-east corner of Route 191 and the Lincoln Highway. I set my bag between my feet, and lifted my thumb. I was on my own, headed north.

Within five minutes, a red Thunderbird stopped. "Well, where you headed, son?" The driver was perhaps ten years older than I was, and he had the boots and the big hat to go with his smile.

"Aiming for Alaska to find work this summer, sir. Name's Steve." I never did get his name, or perhaps he never gave it.

"Well, I can get you the first hundred miles or so along your way, so get on in."

We roared north in the dimming but crystal light, the two-lane asphalt cutting through bunchgrass that seemed to go on forever. Antelope raced along beside the Thunderbird, and occasionally sprang with daredevil leaps across the road ahead of us. As we crossed the Fremont County line, I was regaled by my native host with stories of the bloody wars between cattleman versus sheepherder of only seventy-five years ago. He was clearly partial to the cattlemen's side. "Well, there's a pretty fair roadhouse up ahead a few miles. I'll buy you a Wyoming steak, son."

My host seemed well, perhaps intimately, acquainted with both the waitress-cum-bartender and the surly cook. He introduced me as if we had been long-time buddies, and we two solitary patrons ate two and a half of the biggest (and toughest) steaks it has ever been my pleasure to consume. The roadhouse restaurant-bar consisted of a huge room with peeled wood beams and a lingering aura of what it must be like on a wild Saturday night, out here in the middle of nowhere. We drank what I later came to recognize as "western" coffee: black and watery, as opposed to "cowboy" coffee: black and strong enough to float the spoon. The pie of last season's berries was sweet, juice-drippy, and measured about three wedges to the circle. We bid our hostess adieu. "So long, darlin's, stop by if you get back this way," she waved. We were off, with the sun lying just above the westward ridges.

I asked my host if he knew of a good place along the road up ahead where I could roll my bag out for the night.

"Well, son, it cools down pretty quick at dark around here, but there's this old line shack up ahead a few miles. Only used at the spring and fall round-ups. Nobody will mind if you bed down in there." And, true to his word, he dropped me off just before sunset, in Cowboy Heaven. Then, to my astonishment, he U-turned the 'Bird, and roared back down the way we had come, no doubt to engage the waitress in further conversation.

It was a narrow, well-grassed valley, bordered by aspen rising to the ridges. In the river meadow behind the sagging wooden buildings and empty corrals, cattle and antelope were grazing together, side by side.

The old, slant-leaning bunkhouse itself was rusty and dusty and empty; a broken windowpane was loosely stuffed with a rag. Inside the building was one metal bedframe with a rolled-up old mattress. There was an axe with a splintered handle, and a cast-iron stove, and outside a stack of bone-dry wood stood by the corrals. I split enough of the wood to warm myself against the gathering evening chill. I fired up the stove, priming it with pages from last autumn's *Pinedale Gazette*, rolled my bag out on the mattress, and fell asleep, listening to the scurrying of the kangaroo mice on the bunkhouse floor, the owls hooting in the moon-risen meadow, and the quickening breeze in the aspen. It was June 14, 1957, and my heart was easy in my breast.

I awakened suddenly, disoriented, perhaps with the awareness, or the sixth sense, that something was not right. A pale cottony white light filled the bunkhouse, suffusing everything with a silent glow that was almost, but not quite, luminescent.

I looked at my watch. The hands showed seven-fifteen, but the second hand was not sweeping. I put the watch to my ear, and realized it was stopped; it must have been damaged while I was splitting wood.

Moving over to a grimy windowpane, I saw that the same white light was shining everywhere. Had I died of blueberry pie overdose, and truly woken up in Cowboy Heaven? Apparently not quite yet; for on the ground lay three or four inches of powdery snow, with more coming down by the bucketful. What time was it? Probably at least mid-day, given the brightness of the light. My groggy mind now remembered something half-heard on the radio, was it only yesterday, short of Rock Springs? "Possible late-season blizzard moving up from Colorado." My brain, still set to Eastern time and clime, had refused to register the possibility of a sudden snowstorm in mid-June. But here we were.

I packed and rolled my bag, slipped the poncho over my head (thus exposing the sleeping bag to the falling snow), and felt my way out the twenty yards to the road. Nothing was in sight in either direction through the diminished visibility. No tracks lay on the road; none made by human, animal, or Detroit. Back in the shack, I considered my situation more carefully. While I might get a bit hungry, I had at least a bag of peanuts and half an O'Henry candy bar in my Gladstone, and plenty of stovewood to keep warm by, and to melt snow water. So I was not without food or drink. A car, or a plow, was sure to come through that day or the next, this was the major road between Rock Springs and Jackson Hole. Things would work out; all I had to do was to be patient.

It couldn't have been more than fifteen minutes, with the snow still coming down hard, before I heard the sound of a car grinding up the road from the south. I grabbed my stuff, ran out to the road, and made the foolish gesture of sticking out my thumb, instead of waving my arms.

The car was all black, an ancient Nash, perhaps '46 or '47, with a dent for every mile. Behind it was towed a black flatbed trailer, and atop the trailer was secured, upright, a black Harley-Davidson, equally ancient and dented. The conglomeration came to a stop, skidding a bit beyond me in the powder. The sight presented an ominous and eerie apparition—a world of black on white.

He was all in black as well: black Stetson, black hair, black 'cycle jacket, black jeans, black boots, and black gloves. He was stringy and well-used, and the three days' stubble on his cheeks was, well, black.

He rolled the window down, squinting against the snowflakes and the white light. "Hey, bub, you sure picked a funny day for hitch-hiking. Where you bound?"

"North to Alaska, Mister." The phrase was from the John Wayne movie of the same name, and its theme song, which proclaimed: " North to Alaska. We're going North, the Rush is on!"

"From the looks of this weather, we must be almost up there already, bub. Hop in, I'll take you to Jackson, just twenty miles up this Hoback Canyon road. You can get breakfast there."

"Breakfast? It must be afternoon by now."

"Shoot, bub, it's not even seven-thirty on a beautiful morning in full Wyoming spring conditions. C'mon, hop in."

He looked to me like Jack Palance, the bad black-hatted gunfighter in a number of classic Westerns, or maybe like Richard Boone, the anti-hero hero of the 1950s TV Series, "Have Gun, Will Travel." I don't know if he was a gunfighter or not, but he surely wasn't bad. His name, I kid you not, was, of course, Jim Black, and that old Nash was warm and cozy and full of song and laughter as we skidded and sputtered slowly through the snowy Hoback canyon and came down into the little town of Jackson.

The snow stopped and the sun shone as we drove down the main street, with its many false-front buildings, themselves fronted by wooden boardwalks. Jim slid his rig to a stop in front of the Silver Dollar Bar and Café. "Whoa there. Get yourself the best breakfast in town here, bub. Try the Silver Dollar pancakes."

I offered him breakfast, but he declined. "Got to get this rig up over to Cody for the bike races, and had best be moving along. There'll be snow aplenty time I get to Yellowstone"

"Those races might be quite a goat-rope, if it's snowing as much up there as it was where you picked me up. Thanks, and drive carefully."

Jim laughed, winked, waved a gloved hand, and was gone, whistling one last chorus of "North to Alaska."

I pushed my way in through the bat-wing doors (they might probably be there to this day, if you don't believe me), took a revolving stool at the counter, and gazed down at the rows and rows of silver dollars inlaid all along the counter (which at night was the bar, and no doubt even busier than for breakfast). I left my Gladstone, minus the shaving kit and towel, under the watchful but friendly eye of the grizzled old-timer seated next to me, and cleaned up in the washroom. Then I cleaned up again, this time on the best plate of pancakes and link sausage and (western) coffee I could ever remember eating.

Moving out onto the opposite side of the sunlit main street, I lifted my thumb once again. I had barely time to feel those pancakes begin to settle before a brand-new Volkswagon bus stopped.

Its driver looked like he would be more at home in Olde Lyme, Connecticut than in Jackson, Wyoming. He was clad in khaki 'chinos', an open-necked short-sleeved shirt, and had one of those little plastic thingy's in his breast pocket with several pens, and the obligatory 1950s slide-rule. But, like everyone else in western Wyoming, he seemed to be chronically-infected with Smile Disease. "Where can I take you, my young friend?"

"Name's Steve, and I'm headed north, up to Montana and then to the AlCan for Alaska. Appreciate any lift you can give me."

"Well, I can only get you five miles or so up the road, but at least that's a start out of town, and there's sure to be someone who will be heading north."

We hung a left at the little park in the center of town, the one with arches of elk antlers framing the entry paths, and moved north in the lee of a long bluff to the west.

"That's Gros Ventre, Fat Belly, Butte. A lot of things have French names around here, tagged by the French Canadians who came down into this country after beaver. They were among the first of the Mountain Men. I'm turning off west just after we pass the Butte, over to Warm Springs Ranch."

I suppose the words "Mountain Men" set the fever alight in my brain, and then, as we came up to the end of the Gros Ventre Butte, I saw them in the morning sun, standing to the northwest and front-lighted from the east. I saw them, something lifted up inside me, and I never have been the same, even to this day, forty years and more later.

There they stood, compact in an uneven broken line, glistening crests of rock and snow and ice. They were just a short range, separated from the rest of the chain of the Rockies by flat spaces to north and south, and cut by deep west-running canyons between the peaks. Though you could not, from where we were, see the chain of blue lakes along their eastern front, the green dip of conifers told you the lakes were there.

"What are those mountains, mister?"

"Those, my boy, are the Grand Tetons, and out in front of you is Jackson Hole. The Snake River runs through it. The Mountain Men crossed through the Hole in the 1820s and 30s, looking for beaver, moving back and forth to their yearly rendezvous sites: west of the range in Pierre's Hole, southwest on the Bear River, over southeast on the Sweetwater, and down south of the Hoback on the Green River. They gathered each spring, coming in from wherever they had spent the winter, to trade, to raise hell, and to plan the year's beaver hunts. Jackson Hole was a sort of center-point, a cross-roads on their trails of exploration during the high time of the Mountain Men. They called it a 'shining time', and those are the Shining Mountains. I've always wondered where that phrase came from, though it's plain to see what it signifies. Last year I read that when the French explorer, Pierre La Verendrye, was looking for furs way over north and west of Lake Superior, back in the 1740s, almost a hundred years before the Mountain Men got out here, the Indians told him that far to the west there were mountains 'that shined by night as well as by day.' They had it right, for sure. Just be here in the moonlight, and you'll see."

Thoughts of Alaska vaporized. This was my place.

"Stop the car. I mean, slow down, please. Do you think there might be any work around here, mister? I can do most anything, especially if it's outside."

"Well, I don't know, but there is the National Park headquarters up the road there at Moose, and I think they usually take on seasonal help for the summer. Tell you what, I'll run you up to the park, past Moose Junction, it's just a few miles further on than I was going anyway, and you can try your luck."

We drove through the valley of Jackson Hole, elk and trumpeter swans to the right of us in the National Wildlife Refuge. The visual passage was clear to the north, and always the peaks lay to the west. We dipped down to cross the Snake at Moose Junction, passing the Chuckwagon, a tourist restaurant under tent canvas, with huge grates and cauldrons already firing up. At the Chuckwagon, I came to learn, if it was made of beef, you could order it. If it wasn't made of beef, they were temporarily out of it. Alongside the river lay the log-framed Chapel of the Transfiguration, through whose huge altar window the simple wooden cross was silhouetted against the soaring peaks. On the other side of the road was a small general store, also of peeled logs, with a telephone hung outside, next to a Sinclair Oil gasoline pump.

Once past the river bridge, the road wound up onto a forested benchland fronting the mountains. A sign proclaimed: "Welcome to Grand Teton National Park."

I hopped out, offering my thanks to the driver for going considerably out of his way for my convenience, and walked into the entrance road.

Park headquarters was a cluster of log buildings with green roofs, surrounded by lodgepole pine forest. There was a jumble of jeeps and pick-ups in the central yard, and nobody much was around; it was Sunday morning.

I knocked on the door of the building marked "Central Administration." Being hailed in, I faced a youngish man with a leathered face, a receding hairline, and a nicely-developing beer gut, sitting slouched behind a desk. On the desk was a sign, "Assistant Superintendent." But from under the desk stuck out a pair of well-used, and well-oiled, work boots, and the hand he waved me in with was clean but heavily callused.

"Sir, I was headed for Alaska, but I saw those mountains. Any chance you have work for me? I'm strong and not too bright, and I can do most anything."

"Well (that word seemed to be the way to begin any sentence in these parts; sort of a front-end punctuation mark, like the inverted question mark in written Spanish), we filled our Trail Crews last week, but I had some Eastern kid quit on me this morning, so I do have one place open, and tomorrow is Monday, and Billy Jiggs from Driggs has got to take a crew up on the Hidden Falls Trail. Would you mind working in the woods? You'd have to spend some time in the mountains."

"Well (by now I had become similarly speech-affected), I guess I could do that, if you really need somebody." I am certain he saw right through my affected nonchalance; eagerness must have been all over my face. He tried to suppress a grin.

"Then you're in luck, and we have a deal, young pardner, as long as you are not on the run or some kind of dope fiend, and can sign your name. Just throw your gear over in the bunkhouse, and we can fiddle with Uncle Sam's paperwork tomorrow, early morning. If you're hungry, there's probably some cold pancakes left in the kitchen"

And, as I was backing out the door, he added, "Oh, yeah, by the way, what's your name, so I can tell Billy."

—DICK, JIM, AND THE GHOSTS OF JOHN AND JEDEDIAH —

I carried the Gladstone over across the dusty yard, seeing nothing more animate than a pair of Levi's-clad legs sticking out from under a Chevy truck, and hearing nothing more than the sweet whang of Hank Williams' " Your Cheating Heart", emanating from the truck radio, accompanied by occasional and desultory metallic clangs from under the chassis.

The bunkhouse differed from the other buildings in that its logs were painted white. The screen door banged behind me, and I was immediately standing in the 'dining room': concrete floor with several long white wooden tables with detached white wooden benches; sugar bowls, salt and pepper cellars, and metal napkin dispensers on each table, enough seating to hold twenty or twenty-five hungry people. The kitchen was off to the left, through a door and a large serving window, and what I could see of it looked like a major outfit: enormous cast-iron stove, steam-table and commercial dishwasher, big fridge and freezer, metal counters. The place was quiet and seemed deserted; no meals were served on Sundays.

A round, tousled head peeked out from behind the kitchen door-jamb, and a refrigerator door clunked behind it.

"Hey, whacha dune? Nice morning, huh?" This around a mouthful of pancake.

"Just getting in. Was in Rock Springs yesterday. Terrible place. Name's Steve. Going to work trail crew."

"Hi, I'm Dick Robbins. Chicago (this pronounced just as in the old song: 'Chicken in the car and the car won't go. And that's the way to spell Chicago.'). Want to go fishin'?"

The rest of Dick emerged from around the jamb. He was slightly above middle height, brown hair and eyes, round face, stocky but solid, and moved with fluidity rather than in bursts, kind of rolling smoothly along.

I learned, once I was able to interpret the strange speech ("moo'n pitcher," "chorkorlit"), that Dick was indeed from Chicago, and was at the University of Colorado in Boulder, where he was majoring "in skiing and girls," working as a short-order cook to get by. He thought Chicago was what was left over after they had made the beautiful Rockies, and, after he got expert enough in skiing and girls, his further ambition was to fly airplanes, big airplanes, for the United States Air Force (and, indeed, he did become a Strategic Air Command pilot, spending his career in such garden spots as Minot, North Dakota, flying the B52's). Dick was nothing if not decisive. If it could be climbed, skied, fried, flown, or gently sweet-talked, Dick Robbins was your man for it. It also seemed they had Smile Disease down there in Colorado as well as in Wyoming, and Dick had a bad case of it.

" I got my private pilot's license this year. Maybe we can go flying some time out of the Jackson airport. Should get some wonderful bumps from the thermals in front of the mountains. Fly up to Yellowstone. Fly over the Falls. Take some girls. But today we got to go fishin'."

There was a phrase in my Western novels I really liked: "A man to ride the river with." It took me only about five minutes to figure out that, if there was such, Dick Robbins was it. Nothing rattled him and his good humor. He took reverses and obstacles in the same easy stride as he took good fortune. If there was a tool, he knew how to use it. If there was a problem, he would give it some thought and then go ahead and fix it.

"Let me go upstairs and drop my gear, and I'll be right with you."

"Doncha warnt some pancakes first?"

"No thanks, Dick, I had enough pancakes this morning at the Silver Dollar to last me two days. Check with me in the morning, though. I could be ready."

I went up the wooden stairs at the side of the kitchen, and adjusted my eyes to the dim light under the log eaves. Twenty or so metal bedframes, with mattresses, slipless pillows, and Army blankets, were lined along the two longer walls. Open white-painted wooden lockers, most with clothes on hangers and shelves, stood at intervals and on the inside short wall. Two large windows let light in through the fourth wall, and shaded bulbs were hung from the peaked ceiling. A large, white-painted washroom was at one end, with sinks and mirrors, johns, and showers. There were about a dozen towels on the hooks. I found what appeared to be an empty cot, threw down my Gladstone, and sat for a minute, thinking how far I had come in four days, and how far I had come since the snow in Hoback Canyon just several hours ago. I thought about the Mountain Men, seeing this country for the first time, as I had seen the Tetons just this morning. I wondered if it had felt to them as it had felt to me, and if it had changed something nameless inside them as well.

A soft and liquid voice issued from a cot in a dark corner. "Hi, my name's Larry. From Montana. The Flathead Rez. We're goin' fishin', if you want to come."

"Yeah, great, Larry, that's what Dick said. I'm with you."

"Great. Jim too. He's got the car."

Larry rose soundlessly and effortlessly from the bunk, all five and a quarter feet of him, dark straight hair and dark, dark eyes, and big knotted shoulders. I followed him back down the stairs. His soft footfalls were barely audible; my clumsy boots clunked behind him.

Dick was sitting straddling one of the benches, still chewing pancake, one in each fist. As we went over to him, the bunkhouse door blew open and in came the Wild West Wind.

"Hey. Let's go. Ready? Get a move on, the fish won't wait all day. C'mon, it's past eleven o'clock already. Be dark soon. Head 'em up. Hi, name's Jim, Jim Burdock. Let's go. Bang bang. We won't know what's there if we don't go look."

Jim was about one hundred and forty-five pounds soaking wet, a couple of inches shy of six feet, not an un-oiled joint in his lean whipcord body. He always looked like he was moving fast, but he was really always moving slow, and smooth, and effortlessly. I never have met anybody who gave more the impression that he was in a terrific hurry, while he was really taking his time. He had nondescript brown hair, pale ice blue eyes, and, man , he was the *inventor* of Smile Disease. As I learned later, he could talk you out of your socks (or any other piece of apparel), and was a bit of a devil with the ladies. He had that "Aw, shucks, ma'm, my hand isn't really there" cowboy way that snaps like a mousetrap on (especially Eastern) girls, but he was very quiet and polite about it. Jim had been raised in the Sandhill Country of western Nebraska, a ranch kid, and was a couple of years older than most of us. He had graduated from the University of Wyoming down in Laramie, and spent the past year teaching school over in Dubois (here pronounced Dew-boys), a settlement just over the mountains northeast from Jackson. What he wanted to do with his life was, "Well let's just go look, and see what happens," but, hard as he worked at it, the keen intelligence under his hat was hard to hide. He had the Western hat and the Western boots, and he drove a garbage pick-up truck for the park. Said it was a good job for the summer, because he got to meet a lot of girls in the campgrounds and parking lots.

We headed into the yard, piled into Jim's old rattletrap Ford (made back when you could get any color you wanted, as long as it was black), and, trailing oily smoke behind the black and orange bucking horse Wyoming license plate, turned north on the main park road towards the Jackson Lake Lodge. I was a bit surprised, because nobody seemed to have any fishing gear.

After five or ten miles, when I thought I had better mention that we had forgotten something, Dick looked at Jim, Jim looked at Dick, and Jim said," Well, Steve, here's how we go fishing up here in the Tetons of a Sunday afternoon. First we go up to the Willow Flats below the Lodge, and Larry here will show us how to *really* catch trout. Then, after we cook and eat 'em, and rest a while from our labors, it gets to be about four or five o'clock in the afternoon, and we go up to the bar in the Lodge, and sit there, and have a little drink, and go fishing for the girls who work up there. It's early in the season yet, just beginning, but I think it's going to be a good year. "

This was the second summer in the Park for all three of my companions, so I thought I better just follow along and work it like they said. Sounded good to me.

~

It took us about a half-hour to reach the Jackson Lake Junction. On the way, I got my first look at the crystal blue waters of Jackson Lake, the largest lake in the park. Across the water to the west soared the flat-topped Mount Moran, girdled by glaciers, and with a distinctive oxide-colored natural dike running down its upper east face. Mount Moran was currently best known as the peak into which an airliner had slammed during a winter storm a few years earlier; the bodies and parts of the plane were still up there. The mountain was named after the great early painter of the American West, Thomas Moran. Strangely enough, Moran never saw 'his' mountain from its most dramatic, Jackson Hole, eastern side, but he did get to paint it from the west.

Thomas Moran, a rather mousy and timid-appearing Philadelphia engraver, British-born, had been engaged as the back-up artist on the Hayden expedition of 1871. Led by the Director of the US Geological and Geographical Survey of the Territories, Ferdinand V. Hayden, the expedition set out to document the wonders of the region that included what was to become Yellowstone Park. Moran formed a close partnership and friendship with the expedition's photographer, William H. Jackson, and Moran's watercolors and later-executed oils of the geysers, steaming pools, colored rocks, lakes, and Yellowstone Falls and Canyon, substantiated by Jackson's photographs of the same scenes, created a sensation back East, and at the Centennial Exposition in Philadelphia in 1876. This incontrovertible documentation of the scenic marvels of Yellowstone played a significant part in the creation of our first National Park and the subsequent treasures of our National Park System.

Moran did not accompany the Hayden expedition's foray into Jackson Hole, south of Yellowstone in 1872. He turned further south, to paint the Grand Canyon, but Hayden named Mount Moran in his honor. Moran himself did not see the Tetons until 1879, when, with a military escort, he approached, and painted the range from the western (Idaho) side.

Between the Jackson Lake road junction and the edge of the lake were the Willow Flats, a low and somewhat marshy area where a number of small streams threaded into Jackson Lake. Jackson Lake is, actually, just an extremely wide place in the Snake River, which enters its north end, and flows out through a small dam to the south-east. It was here that I got my first taste (or, more accurately, vice versa) of the big local mosquitoes, or as some called them, the Jackson Hole Canaries. In truth, the tiny no-see-um black flies were much worse, but they weren't about at the moment. Fortunately, there was bright sun and a pretty good breeze, and the Canaries were a relatively minor nuisance for most of this day.

Their specialty, like the Royal Air Force over Berlin, was after the sun went down.

We wandered down along one of the larger streams, lay down in the sun, had a smoke (Luckies and Camels for the locals, Marlboros for the wanna-be cowboys), watched the clouds roll by overhead, and then, when we were good and ready, got down to the serious business of fishing. Dick and Jim had, between them, in their pockets, a half-dozen fish hooks and about twelve feet of line—in six pieces of unequal lengths. The three of us dapped (British fancy fishing language for "dipped") short lines in the water, baited with worms I dug up from the soft soggy ground with my pocket knife. But this was only a diversion from the main event, and we never did catch any trout that way that day.

What really was going on was this: Larry would sneak up to the stream bank, on his belly, absolutely silently. In slow motion he would push his arm over the bank, into the water, and underneath the grassy overhang. Then he would sort of wiggle his fingers in a motion I never was able to master, and that he called "tickling the trout." Jim later told me that what he was actually doing was stroking their bellies, and mesmerizing them. In about 15 minutes he had flipped a half-dozen small brookies onto the bank, and that was all there was to it. I have heard of people catching fish with willow wand rods, reed-woven nets, bows and arrows, and fish spears, but I have never seen anything like that Flathead friend of mine that afternoon. The only thing I could compare it to was in my Western stories, where the young braves would slip in among the pony herd, and steal them silently away, while the enemy camp slept on, unawares.

We gutted and cleaned the trout with our small knives, spitted them on willow sticks, cooked them over a small, smokeless fire right on the stream bank, sucked our greasy fingers clean, and soon were lying, contented, on our backs again, smoking and talking, resting after all that hard work.

I already knew that Jim's job for the summer was driving the garbage truck. Larry, it seemed, was just passing through for a few days, on his way to work on assignment with a fire-fighting crew based up in Yellowstone Park to the north of the Tetons. Dick, it turned out, was a major player on the *real* trail crew. These were the experienced hands who did not come back to Park Headquarters and the bunkhouse each night, but lived for days and weeks at a time high in the mountains, at tent camps or winter refuge cabins, or under the sky, working the back trails in the high country. Their year-round park staff supervisor, Buddy, who was in training to get his deer that next fall by running it down with a hunting knife (and he did it, too; his explanation was that it wasn't so hard, all you had to do was to keep moving after it until the deer became exhausted and lay down), would drop in on them every once in awhile, but they were largely on their own, and had to really know what they were doing. The *other* trail crews, such as the one I would be joining, were regarded by that elite as sort of rear-echelon soldiers.

As we lay there, a little groggy from the sun and the trout, Jim began what I soon was to recognize as one of his school-master-type discourses.

"The reason they call that bay up around the east side of the lake Colter Bay, is in honor of John Colter, probably the first white man, certainly the first American, to come through the Hole. That was in 1807. Colter was the youngest member of the Lewis and Clark Corps of Discovery, 19 years of age (same age as you said you are now, Steve) when he signed on in Missouri. He was kind of a hell-raiser, but also a superb hunter, and became, along with Pierre Drouillard, the main meat-getter and special assignment scout for the expedition.

"When they finally started down the Missouri River for home, in 1806, John decided he didn't want to leave this shinin' country. Guess he saw the mountains like we all did. So he came back upriver on the Missouri, and did a little exploring all by his lonesome. By 1807 a big Saint Louis trader, Manuel Lisa, was sending him out to spread the word to the

Crows and other tribes that the Great White Father's fur-trading super-market was coming. Colter just moved around all this country by himself, with his long rifle and a thirty pound pack. Lived with the Indians in the winter, especially the Crows.

"Colter had a number of run-ins with the Blackfeet; in fact, some blame him for the intractable hostility of the Blackfeet to the Americans, though I guess they were just trying to keep hold of their way of life. The most famous story about John Colter and the Blackfeet is when, one time, the Indians captured Colter and a companion, butchered the other man alive in front of Colter, flung the bloody pieces in his face, and told John to run for his life. He outraced those Blackfeet for five miles or more, turning to kill the one brave that stayed close behind him, with the brave's own spear. Then he hid in the icy-cold Jefferson River all day, poking his nose up beneath some drifting logs and reeds, until the Indians gave up looking for him and went home.

" After he came through the Hole in 1807, he went up north through Yellowstone Park, just like the tourists do today, and saw the steaming pots and geysers and hot springs. When he told about the marvels he had seen, nobody quite believed him, but for years Yellowstone was known to the Mountain Men as 'Colter's Hell.' Many took the stories to be tall tales, such as the one "Old Gabe," Jim Bridger, a leader years later among the Mountain Men, liked to tell: "You could catch your trout in one pool, and boil it for dinner in the pool next door!" said Bridger, who was, of course, not exaggerating.

"What happened to John Colter, Jim," I asked.

"Well, by 1810, this first, most indestructible, youngest, and maybe greatest of the Mountain Men had had enough. He went back to Missouri to farm (can you imagine that?), married, and died two years later of liver disease."

Dick's voice rose from the grass: "John Colter sure was something, but I don't think you can call him the greatest. The greatest was undoubt-edly Jedediah Smith, the Mountain Man's Mountain Man. The beaver were a sidelight to him; what Jed Smith really was driven by was exploration—he discovered South Pass, down below the Wind Rivers, where the wagon trail was later to take settlers over the mountains; he was the first white man we know of to cross the Sierras; he blazed trails all up and down the Rockies, in the dry country beyond, over by the Great Salt Lake, and in California. Jed Smith did more than anyone to understand the geography of the Shining Mountains. What all those early guys were looking for were two things: beaver to trap, and an easy river route to the Pacific, to connect up with the Missouri. They never found that route. This area around the Hole is a kind of a hub from which the water spokes fan out, going east and west from the Continental Divide, but, as Lewis and Clark and many others found out, there is no direct, easy passage. But the idea died hard; for years they searched for the Bonneventura River, which was supposed to flow from the west side of the Rockies through the Sierras to the sea, but they didn't find it, because it didn't exist. They sure found beaver, though, and they trapped the mountain streams, hard, for twenty years or so, until the beaver were all but gone. Then the Mountain Men were all but gone, too. Their entire era lasted from the very early days of about 1810 to only about 1840, when the beaver streams began to be trapped out, and when changes in men's fashions back East and in Europe created a disastrous decline in prices for pelts.

"Jedediah was quiet and religious, but a great leader of men. He had come West with Ashley's brigade as a green youth of twenty-three, and immediately showed his leadership qualities among men older and more experienced than he was. When he formed the Rocky Mountain Fur Company with David Jackson (and by the way, that's who Jackson Hole and the Lake are named for—even though Colter had come through first, years before) and Bill Sublette, they brought about the most efficient and successful fur trapping operation in the Rockies. They were the first to bring goods by wagon into the mountains and to the Mountain Men's rendezvous. Ironically, they probably accelerated the sharp decline in beaver and fur prices that led to the end of what they most loved in these Shining Mountains. There's a Mount Jedediah Smith over on the west side of the Tetons, I've been over there last summer, just to have a look around. It's right next to Mount Meek—over by Alaska Basin—named after Joe Meek, who was one of the wildest of that hair-raising bunch. What a bunch they were, and what a time, a Shinin' Time, that must have been up here. I wish, well, never mind. . ."

"And how did Jed Smith end up, Dick," I asked.

"Well, unlike Colter, he died with his boots on, killed in a fight with Comanches, way down on the Santa Fe Trail, in 1831, at the advanced age of 32. His entire career of exploration and beaver trapping in the Rockies had lasted but a short eight years. He had tried, once, to leave the mountains and settle down, like John Colter did before him, but of course he couldn't do it, so he came back. If there was a "greatest" of the Mountain Men, Jed Smith was it."

"And what about David Jackson?"

"Interesting. Almost nothing is known about Jackson, where he came from, where he went after Jedediah was killed. He first turns up, with Jed, at Ashley's big fight with the Arikaras along the Missouri in the early 1820s. He was with the group traveling the Santa Fe trail when Jed was killed, a decade later. But, before and after, nobody knows. Like that song says, he came with the dust, and he went with the wind. He was judged by his peers to be one of the best brigade leaders of the beaver hunts, knowing just where to go, and how to stay alive to get there, and keep your hair in the process. "

After a bit, the sky clouded over some more, the mosquitoes got bad and the no-see-ums showed up, and Jim announced that it was time "to go up to the Lodge and do some more serious fishing." Larry, who was as shy as a cat at a dog convention, decided to head back on his own to the bunkhouse. It was no trick at all to move easily around the park road system; all summer long the tourists, and the Park Service vehicles, would pick up any young person who stuck his, or her, thumb out, day or night. No one on either side of that Fifties' deal worried about there being any threat to their personal safety. About the only bad thing I ever heard happening was when one of our crew was in a car that bounced off a bear that was crossing the road at night over by Signal Mountain. The bear ran off, but the car had to be towed. Nobody was hurt.

So Jim, Dick and I got back in the Ford. Jim was driving, Dick was in the shotgun seat, and I was in back snugged up between the silent ghosts of John and Jedediah. We meandered up to the Lodge, perched on a bluff overlooking the lake.

I don't remember much about the architecture or interior lobbies of the Jackson Lake Lodge, because I only entered it a few times, and those were to go to the bar. Mostly, as I will relate, the time we spent "at the Lodge" was actually at the recreation hall or single-story dorms for the young college kids who were working there for the summer. They were busboys, waiters and waitresses, maids, outdoor help, etc. What Dick and Jim told me was *really* nice for the Park Service guys like us, was that the ratio of summer workers at the Lodge was about three females to every male. Ah, hah. I comprehended that arithmetic. As I came to understand it, there was kind of a pecking order, a status chain, among the young people. At the top were the Park Service crews (and evidently it didn't matter whether you were roughing it in the mountains or driving a garbage truck, if you had the right stuff). In the middle were the kids working at the lodges and concessions in the park. And at the bottom were those unfortunates who were summer help as 'pseudo-Rangers', the 'Flat Hats' who got to dress up and stand at the campground entry kiosks and sell passes and hand out maps. These unworthies had come all the way from New Jersey, so to speak, to Wyoming, when they could have stayed home and been movie theatre ushers for the summer. As is always the case with young people, the rankings were pitiless. Life is unfair, but I figured it was nicer to be an Alpha than an Epsilon.

The bar was cool, high-ceilinged and large-beamed, and full of dark corners. Jim led us to a table in the darkest corner of all, but one from which, I soon realized, we had the best view of, not the other patrons, but of the staff moving back and forth from the bar and the kitchens. As we moved among the tourists, to our table in our jeans and denim jackets and boots, I wished I could emulate the unconscious swagger of my two buddies, but, being only four days out of Cambridge, Massachusetts, and new to the mountains, I was not confident I could pull it off. I also wished I had a pair of *real* boots and a big hat, like Jim.

"Hi, what can I get for you." Her silly little name tag said, 'Sarah, Pocatello, Idaho.' She had hair the color of October cornstalks, and eyes that matched Jackson Lake. All the rest of her, under the striped apron and above the black flat Capezio shoes, looked equally nice to me. I tried to smile back, and said,"Martini, no olive, just a twist." I have no damn idea why I said that, as I had never before in my life ordered a Martini, but it seemed to go down okay, and she smiled back.

"Bourbon, straight up, with water on the side," said Jim, and Dick said, "I'll have an iced tea."

Well, we had a drink or three, and a couple of hamburgers, and Sarah spent plenty of time around our table. We were about out of both pocket money and time when Dick, who had said the least, but looked around the most, asked Sarah, "Who is that tall girl working those tables over on the other side?" Sarah looked through the dim light, and replied, "That's Kitty."

Dick Robbins said not another word, pushed back his chair, walked across the room, and whispered something quietly in Kitty's ear. She turned absolutely white, then red, then pink. I thought she was going to hit him, but she just took two deep breaths, looked into his eyes, and smiled. Dick smiled back, turned around, came back to the table, and told us, "C'mon, it's time to go. I have to start back up Cascade Canyon to camp before it gets dark, and I won't be back down until Wednesday. We can come up here again Wednesday night. I've arranged it with Kitty."

Sarah, who had watched the byplay, said, looking straight at me, "Sure, why don't you all come back up to the rec hall Wednesday, sometime after six-thirty." She deftly executed a pretty little turn thing, and walked away, slower than slow and twice as sweet.

We got back in the car, noting that John and Jedediah had gone off somewhere, and started south, taking the Inner Loop road that goes by Jenny Lake and the Jenny Lake Lodge, from which Dick would have the easiest access to the Cascade Canyon Trail.

The light was fading now; those glimpses of the lakes that we could get showed surfaces of blackening purple. The meadows around Jenny Lake had hidden their blankets of wildflowers. A few deer stood feeding in a dusky meadow; the buck raised his head as we slowed the car in passing, then bent again to graze, unafraid.

The peaks, beyond the lakes and forest, were also darkening rapidly, losing detail of their outlines. But at their summits, especially where one could make out their southern flanks across the canyons, a glistening, shining pink light of alpenglow flared up for a few minutes, and then vanished.

We dropped Dick off, watching him stride into the twilight, his flashlight still in his hip pocket, and continued on south toward Park Headquarters.

"Well, you've had a history lesson," intoned Jim, dropping into his school-master voice, "now let me give you a lesson in the basic geography of Jackson Hole and the Teton Range."

"Yes, ma'm," I replied. "Fire away. But will there be a pop quiz later?"

"Think of the area as a three-layer cake, standing up on its side. To the east is the valley itself, Jackson Hole, between about six and a half to seven thousand feet above sea level. Actually, to the east of *that*, but not part of our cake, is the forested area rising up to the Continental Divide. There is a lake up there, called Two Ocean Lake, which actually has outflows to both the Atlantic and the Pacific. Anyway, the valley itself has the Snake River running through the middle of it, and is not of too much interest except to the few ranchers (dude and otherwise) who inhabit it, and to the Rockefeller family, who bought up most of it, giving substantial amounts back for the park. At the southern end of the Hole is the town of Jackson, with outlets to the south via Hoback Canyon, and to the west via Teton Pass to the other side of the mountains, where the Mountain Men had their rendezvous site at Pierre's Hole.

"The middle layer of the cake is a chain of lakes, running north and south, sitting in the pine forest. Jackson Lake, which you saw today, is by far the biggest, twenty miles or more in length and three or so in width, and is fed by, actually *is*, the Snake. Jackson can get pretty wild in a storm.

"The other, much smaller, lakes form a loose chain south of the big lake—but their sources are the run-off from the mountains on their west sides, and they are not really fed by the Snake. Leigh Lake, String Lake, and Jenny Lake are clumped and connected, and are some of the most beautiful sights on God's green earth. If you remember the novel, *The Virginian*, by Owen Wister (there's a peak around here named for him, too)—the one where the phrase, 'Smile when you call me that, Mister' comes from, and if you remember the 'Honeymoon Island' where the Virginian and the schoolmarm spent theirs, well, that island lies in Leigh Lake. I forget exactly what it's called now.

"Further down lie scattered smaller lakes: Bradley, Taggert, and down near the south end of the Hole, Phelps lake, where a Rockefeller estate is.

"The third, and westernmost, layer of the cake comprises the mountains themselves. There are a bunch of really big ones: Moran, Teewinot, Owen, the Grand, Middle, and South Tetons (the American Mountain Men called them the Pilot Knobs because of their importance as signposts in the wilderness, but the Big Breasts French name stuck, I'm glad to say), all over twelve thousand feet in height, with the Grand pushing past thirteen thousand seven hundred. Then there are a bunch of 'little' ones between ten and twelve thousand feet high. Since the Valley floor is about six and a half thousand feet, and the distance across the lakes to the peaks is only a couple of miles, there is a tremendous vertical lift, giving the impression of a straight rise to Heaven.

" Between the peaks are deep-cut east-west running canyons, like Cascade, which Dick is halfway up by now. Scattered here and there are tiny glacial lakes, with names like Solitude, Icefloe, and Snowdrift, and Forget-Me-Not.

"On the west side of the peaks is a high, desert-like plateau, which forms the park boundary, and which slopes off to the forest to the west.

"And that is pretty much it: full of flowers and wildlife (big and little), and enough room to roam around in so that you can have this cake and eat it, too. More tourists than not just roar on by on the big road, looking for Yellowstone and the bears, and we don't mind letting those ones go. You're around this place for a while, you get to feeling that it kind of belongs to you, or maybe you belong to it, or something like that."

— — —

It was pretty well dark when we got back to Park Headquarters, and the lights were on in the upper story of the bunkhouse. Jim led me up the stairs. Larry was snoring quietly in his corner. A half-dozen others were scattered, reading (mostly Westerns) on their bunks, or playing cards or writing letters. Jim introduced me around: there was a big and rotund, but not fat, guy named Paul from Connecticut, two sort of wiry Tweedledum and Tweedledee mountain climbers from Washington state, and Rod and William ("not Bill, William").

Rod Lane was from a working ranch down near Fort Collins, Colorado. Rangy build, open face, and naïve in the extreme. Kept pictures of his girl and his mom next to his bunk. Didn't swear, smoke, drink, or chase Jackson women, but he did, as I was to later learn to my pride and my grief, "ride rodeo." Rod was on my trail crew, and he could work slow and forever without resting. Said about forty words a day. Shined his boots every night.

William Ward was an older man, about fifty, one of the several I met that summer who were 'left over' from the Great Depression. He had been on the road, and on the rails, hard, during the Thirties, and just never lost the habit. As had many others like him, he had spent a lot of time sitting in public libraries during inclement weather. William was one of the best-read men I have ever met, and he could talk history with you until the sun came up. He hated Hoover, cops, railroad bulls, and "Wall Street bankers." He loved FDR, and Andrew Carnegie (for the libraries). There was, of course, something sad about him, something lost, but he was a polite and gentle soul. He had never married, and once he said to me as I got out of the shower, and we were alone in the washroom, "You know, you look like a Michaelangelo statue." Well, I knew I didn't, and I sort of kept a careful distance from William after that, but I loved to hear him talk about the things he had seen, and the places he had been. He worked on the road (as opposed to the trail) crews, patching asphalt and driving a dump truck, kept to himself at night, reading and smoking in his bunk.

Some of the made-up bunks were still empty, their owners down in Jackson or up at one of the park's lodges, squeezing the last drops out of Sunday.

There was one bunk, over in a corner, that had no mattress, no pillow, no blankets on it, just the bedspring. I asked Jim what that was about.

Jim winked at me. "Well, that's the one we save in case the weather gets really horrid, and Jed or John or Davy or Tom Fitzpatrick, or Joe Meek or Jim Beckwith, or one of those guys, needs to come in and bed down. They don't often do that, because being under a roof and between walls makes them feel closed-in. But if they do, they walk awfully quiet in their moccasins; you won't be disturbed, and they'll be gone before dawn."

Since I couldn't get sheets until Monday, I rolled my sleeping back out, one more time, on the mattress of my bunk, stashed my gear in a vacant cubby, had a last smoke, and turned in. My dreams were colorful and sweet, of the lakes and mountain peaks, of my new friends, of the old Mountain Men, and a little bit of Sarah.

~ BILLY JIGGS & THE HIDDEN FALLS TRAIL ~

I awoke in the pre-dawn half-light, roused by the scurrying, thuds, rustles, muffled curses and suppressed laughter of young men in a barracks or bunkhouse: finding their gear, throwing water on their faces, ambivalent between the urge for more sleep, and the prospect of a good breakfast.

Descending the stairs, I found the latter in full swing, with the formidable Mrs. Green in complete charge. On the menu was just the usual light Continental breakfast fare: pancakes and syrup, fried eggs, bacon, toast, butter, three kinds of jam, watery orange juice, (cowboy) coffee, all in whatever sequence, quantity and repetition one desired. I introduced myself politely to Mrs. Green (whose middle name was undoubtedly Motherhen), knowing full well which side my bread was buttered on, raising my voice to make myself heard above the tumult of young (and not so young) voices debating the achievements, connubial and otherwise, of the weekend just past.

"Darlin'", she said, in a voice which cut through the competition, and which went well with her six feet of height and somewhere around one hundred eighty pounds, "it's nice to be able to welcome another one of you sweet boys to the mountains. Corey (for Corey Green was the name of the assistant superintendent who had hired me on yesterday) told me you looked like you needed a little fattening up, and that's where I come in. You eat up and run along quickly now and get signed in, and when you come back this evenin' we can have a nice chat and get to know each other." I wasn't sure whether Corey was son or spouse, Mrs. Green's aspect and energy being boundlessly ageless. I was already getting the drift that very little that was known to anyone on the permanent park staff was not known as well to *everyone* on the permanent park staff, and also that there were complicated woven threads of interconnected responsibility—and privilege—among them. "And when you grab your sack lunch from that bench by the window, take the sack on the left, it's got just a little extra in it."

I bolted my breakfast, taking little part in the discussions around me, grabbed the sack on the left as instructed, and ran across the yard and into the Central Administration office, just as Corey Green was settling behind his desk. Just like Saint Nick, he said not a word but went straight to his work, and in the next 30 minutes I filled out more brown and white forms attesting to everything from my vital statistics, my work and life history, my loyalty to the Republic, and then some, than I would have ever imagined possible.

Baptised via a set of thumb prints, I evidently made the grade, for Corey Green then swore me in as an official United States National Park Service Temporary Summer Employee, GS Grade 4, Grand Teton National Park, Category: Manual Unskilled Labor. I was to be paid the princely sum (at least it seemed so to me) of two dollars and twenty cents an hour, for a forty hour week, no overtime. Tools and transportation in connection with my work would be provided me. I was to furnish my own clothing and other essentials. Of special note, I was to reside in the park bunkhouse, where three meals a day (breakfast, dinner, and a sack lunch) were to be provided me, no meals furnished on Sundays, and where my "found" included a bunk and weekly towel and linens. In exchange, thirty-five dollars per Federal biweekly pay period were to be extracted from my paycheck, in addition to Social Security. The thirty-five dollars represented almost precisely twenty percent of my pre-tax salary, and I found myself uncharitably wondering how this amount was distributed among Mrs. Green, perhaps *the* Greens, and the United States National Park Service.

"Mr. Green . . . "

"Son, you can either call me Corey, or Your Royal ASSistant Exalted Park Superintendent, whichever you prefer."

"Corey, you told me yesterday that I would be working under Mr. Billy Gripps. What does he look like, and where can I find him?"

"Its Jiggs, Billy Jiggs, with two g's and a j, Billy Jiggs from Driggs, and I suggest you don't *never* call him Mister. Don't worry, Son, Billy knows all about you, and you won't need to find him, he'll find you. Now get a move on and get outside. I have President Eisenhower's work to do behind this goddamn desk, and you don't want to be late for round-up."

I stepped into the early light of the yard, saw small groups of young men, all carrying brown paper lunch sacks, moving towards tools and trucks. I looked right, and then left, and then I felt a callused hand grip my right shoulder, turning me around with about the same easy leverage he would use to move a horse out of the way in a stall.

"Well, you must be Steve, so I must be Billy Jiggs, from Driggs. Welcome to the Tetons and to the crew building the best-by-damn laid-out and constructicated trail in the whole-fired park, or at least it had better be when we get her done. We been working on the Hidden Falls Trail since last summer, takes so much time we ought to call it the Hold Your Balls Trail, and a whole week of this season has gone by already and we ain't even got to the really hard part yet. Maybe some of you sprouts who survive working with me this summer will have to come back again next year and help me finish her. Glad to see you, Son. That guy from back East you're replacing got tired of not having a Dairy Queen handy on the trail, so he went home to Momma. I'm half horse and half alligator, and all lumberjack, and I'm here to help you, but I. Surely. Am. Not.Your. Mother. You remember that and we'll get along just fine."

How to describe a force so elemental, a substance so rock-solid? Billy Jiggs was about five feet nine and two hundred pounds, and I would guess he had about as low a body fat content as a twelve-year old rooster in a busy hen house. If you took a big, full-grown Ponderosa pine, and cut it off cleanly, leaving a stump five feet nine inches high, then you would have Billy Jiggs. Nothing bulged on his arms and legs, it was all just solid, compact, and dense. You had the feeling that the electrons in his constituent atoms didn't spin around much; they were just packed in together too tightly to move very far.

His face was round, but nothing hung down off the edges, despite his forty-five or more years. Grey eyes, grey thinning hair, sun and smile lines on his leathery, creased face. Strong, but not hairy, hands, blunt-edged fingers (a joint or two missing here and there from timber work in the woods up in Oregon), straight-across well-kept nails. Always in fresh blue work clothes that never seemed to wrinkle, because, though he could work like a demon, and lift like Mike Mulligan's Steam Shovel, I never saw him sweat. An old pipe in his mouth which was seldom lit, but the stem not chewed. Hard-worn work-boots, but they were better kept than any I have ever seen. Billy M. Jiggs (I think the M stood for mass).

"Pleased to meet you, Mr. Ji . . . I mean, Billy. What do you want me to do?"

"Just go over there with those boys picking up the tools, generator, rock drill, and dynamite, help 'em throw all that stuff in the truck, and climb in the back on top of them. You and I will have a little chance to talk when we get to Jenny Lake."

I threw in some shovels, axes, two-man cross-cuts, and pulaskis (a tool developed by forest firefighters, with a vertical narrow axe blade on one end of the head, and a horizontal mattock blade on the other. You could cut roots, branches, and small trees with the first, and scrape earth, dig trenches, and pry out stones with the second. The pulaski is the best tool ever developed for cutting trail or fighting fire in rocky forest), and I left the dynamite-hefting to other, more experienced, hands. You can bet I climbed pretty gingerly into the truck bed, being as careful where I set my nether parts as a cat walking on thumbtacks.

Here is what I learned about Billy Jiggs from the other guys on the crew, as we jounced and bounced in that open truck bed on the road to Jenny Lake that beautiful Wyoming morning.

He had been a combat infantry sergeant in the War, from Normandy onwards, and you could see immediately why men would follow him. He would never talk about the war, no matter how he was asked, just give his half-smile and say, "That was a long time ago."

He lived, where he was born, in the little hamlet of Driggs, Idaho, just on the other side of the mountains. It seemed like everybody in that town (and that was not a big number) was named either Jiggs, or Driggs, or occasionally Griggs. Billy had a small farm and a few head of cattle, and three big young sons, of whom he was lovingly proud, helping him work it. I got a sense of why he felt that way one day, later in the summer, when one of the Jiggs boys rode into our lunch break on his horse. The big Appaloosa looked like a Shetland pony under the size and weight of Jiggs the Younger. He had come a day-and-a-half up Teton Creek, over the passes, and down Cascade Canyon to our side of the range. He made the trip just to see his Dad (who hadn't been able to get home that previous week-end), to enjoy the country, and to deliver to Billy a fresh pie from home, which Billy promptly shared with the whole crew. The boy, who was about my age, stayed with us through lunch, speaking not much, but well, and always politely. He kissed his Dad, saddled up, and then rode back over the mountains.

Small-farming and ranching on the Idaho west side of the Tetons didn't have much cash attached to it, so each summer Billy worked as a crew supervisor for the park, much in demand because of his skills with tools and men, and his knowledge of the woods. He had spent several years as a 'jack in Oregon as a young man, and he had plenty of stories to tell about that, as opposed to World War Two. Many of his tales were scarcely believable, as tall as the timber, which I'm told grows pretty tall up there.

Not a man on that crew, nor any I met that summer, had a bad word to say about Billy Jiggs, but there were some things to watch out for.

"Don't pay any attention to it when he cusses you," said Rod, "no matter if he uses words you never heard before. Don't fret at all if he yells and hollers, and jumps up and down, which gives him great pleasure. But if his voice gets real soft, so soft you have trouble hearing it, almost like a whisper, then watch out, back off, and wish you were somewhere else, far away."

"Don't ever let Billy see you put a partner in danger by the way you swing a tool, and you'd better be ready to jump right up back to work when he blows the whistle after lunch," added Paul.

"Don't never let him hear you smart-mouth about the park, the mountains, or the United States of this America," interjected a third person, whose name I hadn't learned yet.

It was pretty simple. He actually didn't have much control over it. Everybody wanted to do their damndest to please Billy, not because of who he was, but because of what he was. My guess was that it had been the same way in Europe, when some of those young men died the hard way for him, and that he knew this, and that was why he didn't want to talk about it.

———————

If you have never seen nor felt an early morning in June in the Rockies, from Montana to New Mexico, you had better run and try to before it's too late for you. It isn't the blue sky or the few puffs of pure white clouds, which may grow to be fearsome dark thunderheads late in the day. It isn't even an almost moist coolness that strokes your cheek, that may well be throat-tightening dusty hot dryness by noon. It's more some combination sensation we have no name for, that is part smell, part feel, and part seeing. It convinces you once and for all that this Earth is precious and beautiful. It was that way on the road to Jenny Lake that morning.

The thin strip of asphalt wove between the dark green lodgepole pines, which were beginning to shine in the early sunlight. At intervals you could glimpse a snowy peak, sometimes tunneled down a long straight stretch of road. Our truck was weaving, too, back and forth over the high crown of the narrow road. Billy was driving, and mostly using both hands to illustrate the points he was making to the two of our guys crammed into the cab with him. He steered by jamming his massive thighs up under the wheel. As we swung back and forth, with the intermittent pothole bumps for good measure, I could imagine those sticks of dynamite rolling back and forth under the tools we were sitting on in the truckbed.

The meadows were carpeted with flowers. To tell the truth, I can't remember well which varieties came into bloom at what point in the short growing and blooming season, but there were floods of blue flax, golden pea, mountain aster,western wallflowers, rabbit brush, shooting stars, evening stars, calypso, mariposa, and penstemons, penstemons, penstemons, coloring the course of the summer in the meadows, woods, and marshy lake margins. The roads were so thickly lined with Indian paintbrush, Wyoming's state flower, that even Custer would have been surprised. To the south of Jenny Lake, in the area called Lupine Meadows, there was an intricate Oriental carpet covering the ground so thickly you could hardly see the tall grass.

Morning was birdsong time: liquid chirps and riffs of thrushes, finches, kildeer, grosbeaks, juncos, and flickers, plus a score of others. Hoarse cracks of Whiskey Jacks and Steller's Jays. Cawing overhead of crows and the big wise magic ravens. Hummingbirds defending their territories, buzzing and squeaking in the red flowers. And more, more than you could identify.

Deer were common, especially at dawn and dusk. Porcupines were come upon, especially at night, lumbering through the brush or climbing the trees. In the marshy shallows of the smaller lakes, moose with enormous hat racks stood, water and green plants dripping from their great lumpy jaws. Bears, as we shall see, were not strangers. The coyotes all went to bed at dawn, but they were a source of lunatic music every night. And I've left out the cottontails and jackrabbits, and the chipmunks, and the many sorts of rodents, and, well, you get the idea. Because of the short lateral distances between great differences of elevation and of dryness, you would move through half a dozen climatic and life mini-zones in a morning's walk, catching a glimpse of a sleek wet otter on a lakeside log at six am, and being chafed at by a rock pika on a dry treeless rockslide before eight.

Billy pulled the truck to a stop at the old boat landing on the near northeast shore of Jenny Lake. He jumped from the cab, came around to the side of the bed, and put his hands on his hips, chest out, chin up.

"Well, you worthless, hung-over, wrung-out, pussy-whipped, incompetent, three-legged, lazy, wet behind the ears sonsabitches, get outta that truck and move your ass and the gear down into the boat before I put that TNT where it will do the most good and where the sun never shines. Rod, you drive the boat to the trailhead across the lake; me and Steve here are going to take a nature walk around the longer way and have a little talk about the birds and bees. When you get to the other side, Ralph and Jerry, you carry the generator. Harry, hump the rock drill— (voice getting much softer) that's what you damn get for dropping it on Friday. Come back for the rest of the hand tools, but you can leave a good load for Steve and me to pick up as we come by after you. Leave the dynamite in the boat, we'll get it later when we need it. Be sure to cover it good with a tarp, case it rains this afternoon. And, goddam it, don't forget the gas can. Again. Everybody got it? Meet you where we left off on Friday. Now, get moving."

Nobody saluted, but everybody said, "Yes, sir, Billy." With dispatch, they piled it all, and themselves, into the open aluminum 24-footer at the wooden dock. Rod jerked the starter cord a few times, and they were gone in a cloud of smoke and a Hearty Hi-Yo Silver.

I felt like Little Red Riding Hood, about to go out for a morning stroll in the woods with you-know-who, but Billy just smiled at me.

"Those are pretty good boys, but they need a little encouragement to get their juices flowing on a Monday morning. 'Sides, they expect me to yell them up that way, would be disappointed if I didn't. But, goddam it, don't get any ideas that I'm easy. You don't want to find out otherwise the hard way. C'mon, let's beat 'em to the junction."

We strode out at a reasonable pace. Billy explained to me, very slowly and clearly, what we were about. "Think of beautiful Jenny Lake as an oval clock-face, north end at twelve o'clock. The Jenny Lake Lodge is up at twelve o'clock, along String Lake, and that old boat dock, where we just were, is nearby, say at one o'clock or so. The old Jenny Lake trail circumnavigates the lake along the water's edge, about seven miles worth. At nine o'clock, Cascade Canyon comes into the lake near Inspiration Point. We are going to need considerable Inspiration, but more Perspiration, to finish that goddam hairy bastard of a trail this summer. The new trail, the one we're building, runs from seven o'clock to nine, in a distance of about two miles. It is, or will be, much higher above the lake, somewhat parallel to the old trail, maybe one-fifty to two hundred feet up, and runs through forest and goddam rockface, which is why the dynamite and drill. The trail will come out, if we ever get the blessed thing finished, at Hidden Falls, so-called because you can't see the falls from the lake itself, as they are hidden behind a rocky knob at the canyon mouth. And, by the way, we have to go over the blasted knob, which blast is what we're going to do to it, because it is solid rock. So, Steve, we're now walking on the lower trail around the lake, and when we come to the junction with the new trail, near the Moose Ponds, we'll head on up it and meet the boys at the point of work, after picking up a load of tools at the junction. Got it?"

"Got it, Billy, sounds great."

"Great? Great, Hell. It is one mother bear flaming sonnavabitch that has got us five ways to Sunday, and every which way but loose, trying to get it done. Hauling all that gear up the steep and narrow, blasting every couple of feet, digging out the Ponderosa stumps and roots, getting to the other side of the lake twice each day, and suckling you sprouts, has driven me Grey, not Great. But we'll get her done, you can bet your sorry ass."

"I'm sorry, Billy, I just meant . . . "

"I know what you meant. And it is great. And don't never again say you're sorry to me."

Billy then commenced to ask me questions about who I was, where I came from, and what my experience was. He generally received my answers without comment, but when I told him I was at Harvard (a fact which I often went to lengths to conceal, or evade, that Wyoming summer), he exploded: "Jeeesus Christ on a Crutch. I wouldn't have guessed it and I'm sorry to hear it. We had one of those worthless bastards from that fairy farm out here a couple summers ago, and he didn't have the sense to pour piss out of his boot before he stuck his foot in it. Well, maybe you're different. We'll see. What kind of work have you done outside?"

"Well, I was a groundskeeper at a summer camp a couple of years back. Built and painted fence, general chores, picked corn for two hundred people twice a week, rolled tennis courts, lined ball fields, swept out the hall, threw around benches, stuff like that."

"Sonny, this ain't no summer camp, and there aren't any tennis courts in the mountains."

"Last year I worked construction down in Miami in the summer. We were building concrete pilings to drive for sea walls. Hot as blazes.

Had a weekly schedule: lay out the cages in the long wooden forms on Monday, Tuesday, and Wednesday. On Thursday, pour the concrete (as the junior guy, I got to carry the cement sacks one after another all day long to the edge of the cement mixer, which moved along the forms, and got further and further away from the shed as the long day progressed. The sacks weighed sixty pounds each, and I went home grey-dusted in all my cracks and crevices), On Friday, help the crane operator lift and align the 30-foot pilings in stacks (without getting your fingers squashed, or getting blown off the high stack by a crane-swung errant piling), and start all over again the next week. It was hot, and I loved it. Got two dollars an hour because I was white; the colored guys only got one seventy-five."

"Well, that sounds a little more like it. We'll see. Ever do any work with the axe?"

"Uh, let's see, a little while ago I was splitting wood down south of here." That was certainly the major misdirecting exaggeration of the year of 1957.

"Well, we'll see. Maybe we can teach you something. What do you want to do with your life?"

"I'm planning on becoming a doctor."

"Is that so. Well, you'll likely learn some things up here that they don't teach you in medical school. Maybe you can change your mind and become a timber bum. I bet they don't teach that at Hahvad."

Here are just some of the things I learned from Billy Jiggs over the succeeding weeks:

How to keep edged tools clean and sharp, and why.

How to use an axe and go home with all your, and your partners', toes attached to feet.

How to measure twice, so you only have to cut once.

How to use a two-man cross-cut saw to fell a big tree just where you want to drop it, without jerking your partner off his feet, and how to keep on your own feet if the bastard jerks you.

How to drill a hole in a crooked rock, straight, the first time.

How to make a big bang, have rocks fly up in the air, and laugh all the way home.

And, how to know that you can get it done, whatever it is, and whatever it takes.

These are lessons that have served me well, my whole life, timber bum or otherwise.

———

We moved up the new trail, me puffing along like a tool-carrying porcupine, and Billy whistling and looking around under twice my load. As we passed through clearings in the pines, the sun was warm on my face, and to our right you could see more and more of the glistening surface of Jenny Lake below. The morning chill and the little mist had risen from the water, and she was now clean, and deep, and endlessly bluegreen, like a giant emerald.

We came around a big boulder sheltering beneath an even bigger tree, and suddenly, though we couldn't see any movement, we heard the clang of shovels against rock up ahead. A few feet further on, we were in the midst of a half-dozen young men in motion, making the dirt fly, and tossing small rocks and stones downhill.

It is only because I soon learned the trick myself, that I am certain as certain can be that a moment earlier, until they heard us, or rather heard Billy, coming up the trail, they were all in full reclining position, faces stretched to the sun and sky, elbows cradled under their heads.

"Alright you motherless polecat whelps, I am glad to find you for once hard at work, unusual as that is. Now you see the marks we posted Friday for the next hundred yards, and for this morning we don't have any stumps or rocks to blast in that distance, so get at it, cut that section level and neat and steady on the rise, and get it done by noon or neither you nor I will eat Mrs. Green's salty sandwiches today. And no smokin' until break, which you have had plenty of already. You bastards can't fool

Billy Jiggs from Driggs. Steve, just let me get these no-brain helpless ficker-wingered cockatoos started, so they don't wander off and fall in the lake, and then I'll show you, if you're capable of learning, what we're doing here."

Billy Jiggs had a hard time watching others work if he couldn't join in himself, and he and everyone fell to, with me trying to imitate their actions as best I could, while the sun rose higher and warmed our shoulders. Soon shirts were off, and those who had caps put them on.

As the pack of earth-eaters moved forward, Billy Jiggs absolutely astonished me, not for the first time, and certainly not for the last. In a resonant clear baritone that echoed off the hillside and lake, he began to sing, and the crew responded:

> Hey, buddy, can't you LINE it?
> Hunh
> Hey, buddy, can't you L-I-N-E it?
> Hunh (with the shovels and pulaskis coming down hard)
> Hey, buddy, can't you li-eye-eye-NIT?
> (and all now together) Way-HAY over that hill.

I came to understand that Billy knew them all—Negro spirituals and prison work songs, old Wobbly (International Workers of the World) union songs from the great Northwest lumber camps, barroom and whorehouse dittys, Big Rock Candy Mountain hobo songs, train songs, and all the rest. And now I know them, too.

Sometimes he would sing the odd verse or two. Sometimes he would mix in verses from two or three songs at once. And sometimes he would regale us with all forty-eleven verses from three different versions of the same song, suitably scatalogically modified.

At lunch break, he could lean back against a tree, and softly, sadly, sing those old lonely Western ballads, the ones where the dying young cowpoke says he wants to be buried with his horse.

I ride an old Paint, and I lead an old Dan,
I'm off to Montana to throw the Houlihan.
Ride around, little dogies, ride around them slow,
The fiery and the snuffy are rarin' to go.

Their tails are all matted, their backs are all sore,
There's water in the coulee, there's feedin' in the draw.
Ride around, little dogies, ride around them slow,
The fiery and the snuffy are rarin' to go.

Old Bill Jones had a daughter and a son,
One went to Denver, the other went wrong.
His wife got killed in a barroom fight,
Still, that cowboy, he keeps singin' from morning to night:

Ride around, little dogies, ride around them slow,
The fiery and the snuffy are rarin' to go.

None of us on that crew ever talked about how we would sing with Billy, up there above Jenny Lake. It was our secret, all together.

We had another secret, too, one we didn't share with others, and of course would never mention to Billy: when he needed to consult the map (which was rarely), Billy would pull out and put on his wire-rimmed spectacles.

<hr>

"Okay, Steve, here's the way she works, here's how you build trail in my Tetons.

It's harder on a steep hillside, like this one is, and where there is lots of rock so you can't dig back in deep for a level, but it works out all the same: what you gotta do, you just do it.

"Making the trail wide enough is easy, at least if you keep at it, and leveling it off within the trail edges is just work, sometimes you have to *add* dirt instead of taking it away, and sometimes you have to fill holes with rocks.

"But the two hardest things you gotta do, and not being in your hydramatic shift truck on Main Street with a surveyor's transit and a thermos of hot coffee makes them harder, are: to keep your line straight and your curves gentle and smooth, so some drunken cowboy doesn't fall all over his feet trying to stay on your trail, and to get your grade going uphill or down steady and not too steep or too shallow, so that same drunken cowboy doesn't fall off and break his fool neck. You never, ever, want to sacrifice an inch by going down when you want to go up, unless you absolutely have to, and vice versa, so you have to eyeball it ahead, plan how your cut will look, measure twice and cut once, and learn to get it just right. When you are cutting switchbacks, it makes the figuring even harder, but it is not rocket science. When you see a well-laid out and well-cut trail, it is a surely beautiful thing. Unfortunately, most of the greenhorn pansies from Boston and Harvard and such that are gonna walk this trail of ours in the next fifty years will never think to look down, unless they are tripping over their shoelaces. But you and I and the boys will know that it was done right.

"Them's the basics. Now I can show you later about cutting tree limbs so those same greenhorns don't poke their eyes out, or, more important, so that the horses don't get spooked, and how to lay water diversions with stones and logs diagonally across the trail so it won't wash out by next Spring, and such like that. And I can show you better than tell you about how to use which tool without giving somebody a short haircut, and that's about it."

And lucky it was for me, too, that on that first day of mine in the mountains we were working a relatively easy stretch of trail. It wasn't too thickly forested, so there weren't many big stumps to dig out or trees to take down. It wasn't bouldered, so we had no grunting, groaning, or dynamiting. It wasn't too steep a rock and shale face, like some of the almost-cliff along the route. All that good stuff was to come later. But that first day was mostly soil, with small stones, an occasional tree root, and lots of sunshine.

That gave me plenty of time to get comfortable with the tools and with my buddies on the crew. I grew to truly love the pulaski, which offered all the subtleties and variety of a fine violin, and required a virtuoso's skill, to which I vainly aspired, to know best how to use what part of it for a given task. The long-handled shovel was an old friend, but learning to skim a flat cut without blunting the edge on a rock was a new challenge. I was only mildly retarded in axe handling, and that day the trees were small, and the roots best left to the pulaski. We had no need that day for the two-man cross cut saw, that living devil from Hell, sent to earth to try men's souls, and to inspire them to new heights of profanity. And the big pneumatic rock drill and its generator, and the dynamite, remained mysteries still hidden behind the veil.

By the end of the day (I don't remember lunch, or what was in the extra-special sack) I was whipped, sunburned, sore-shouldered, low-lidded, and unsteady on my pins. I had painful blisters on my palms, but was glad I had chosen not to wear gloves (especially any that might be marked with the Harvard emblem). My hands would harden up, as would the rest of me.

Because he knew I was raw and tired, Billy graciously allowed me to carry the rock drill, all forty pounds of it, down the hill. You had to balance its four-foot length on your shoulder like a 30 caliber machine gun, and hold your other arm out for balance. Going back down at the end of the day, it was a matter of young male pride that we didn't use the trail (even though we had built it), but rather slipped, skidded, and slid as perpendicularly as possible down the loose rock and debris between us and the lake, whooping and hollering all the way. Skateboards hadn't been invented yet, but if we'd had them, we'd have used them. For me, all that came later; I didn't do much whooping and hollering that first day. Mostly I just tried to pick my way down, avoiding being sent ass over teakettle by the balanced (or unbalanced) rock drill, alternately praying and cursing under my breath, and fighting a distressing tendency of my eyelids to close. I didn't drop the drill, because I knew that if I did, Billy would have me carry it up the hill the following morning.

The ride back across Jenny Lake, the glory of the meadows in the lengthening shadows, the unupholstered jouncing truck back to park head-quarters—I have little recollection of that first experience.

I slumped my way into the bunkhouse, intercepted in the dining room by Mrs.Green. Idly noting for the first time that her strawberry-blond hair was a wig, I made my excuses for not being really hungry for dinner ("because of the splendid lunch"). She seemed to be quite famil-iar with this first day syndrome, just saying, "It's alright, Honey, it will be better tomorrow."

I crept like a rheumatic monkey up the stairs, on all fours, and fell on my bunk fully clothed.

But just before my lights went out, I would swear that I caught, out of the corner of my eye, a flash of old Jedediah, cross-legged in his buck-skins on that empty bunk, his long rifle across his lap, and his clay pipe in his mouth, smiling through the wreath of smoke. He cocked his head at me, and winked, as if to say, "Good boy, old son!"

It had been a Shinin' day in the mountains.

~ SARAH, KITTY, AND THE THREE BEARS ~

By Tuesday evening, and certainly on Wednesday, I began to feel the Hidden Falls Trail reaching up on me through the soles of my work boots, talking to me and me to it, getting the sense of what we were trying to do together. I began to call her "her," just like Billy and the boys did, caressing her with our tools when the going was sweet, hacking and cussing when we were in a hard place, like needing to use the cross-cut on a big ponderosa or spruce where other, smaller trees were clustered around too close to give you a smooth draw. I'd even gotten easy enough with the work load to spend a few minutes of the morning break scouting up ahead a few hundred yards, looking at what our future held for us.

From where we were working, along the hillside on a north-south face, you didn't have much of a view of the peaks, but every once in a while we would work around a corner of the slope, and there they always were, watching us watching them. There was still plenty of snow and ice up high, which shone like diamonds in the June sunlight.

I could guess that by early July we would reach the hardest section of the remaining ground to cover—a steep rocky face with few trees, large boulders, and no shade, with irregular rocks underfoot. Much of that section would have to be blasted, hammered off, and shoveled away stone by stone to create a level trail. There would also be a need to carry in dirt from as nearby as possible, to create a walkable surface. After that would come a longer section in deeper woods that would try our skills with axe and cross-cut saw, and then, if we could get there this summer, the final climb over the rocky knob and around the bend to Hidden Falls.

But for the next few weeks it was almost like practice, or Spring Training, a little bit of everything, but nothing too hard. We'd lay the line (or, rather, Billy would), take out the few trees necessary to remove, chop out roots that would otherwise trip the future unwary pilgrim, pry out the stones and occasional bigger rocks as required, fill and level with earth and small stones, skim off and tamp down the new trail, digging it well back into the slope to keep it broad and level, and add the amenities as we went. We might lay a big log (a just-downed tree with its branches lopped off by an axe) alongside the trail as a convenient rest-stop, always trying to do this in an otherwise shady place. We would build water conduits diagonally across the trail with small stones or half-buried logs, channeling the water flow that was each early spring's enemy to trail preservation. If there was a short, steep incline, we might even set in cut logs to retain earthen steps, so the traveler could keep a steady stride. Billy was always reminding us to think of ourselves walking "our" trail, humping fifty or sixty pounds of backpack up (or what can be even harder, down) the trail, and to put refinements in with thoughts always in mind of the comfort and safety of those who came after. We would vie with each other as to who could think of the neatest trail trick, such as laying a sitting log in front of a just-right-sized small boulder, so the hiker could ease the weight of his backpack onto the rock, as he sat down on the log, without having to take the pack off and then lift it on again.

We moved fast, yards and yards per hour. The weather was good, and we began to function as a crew, rather than as a group of individuals.

It was easy going, and the half-hour lunch break was often ended by Billy leading a sweet song, like the everlasting "Big Rock Candy Mountain."

On a summer day, in the month of May, a burly bum come hikin',
Travelin' down that lonesome road, he was looking for his likin'.
As he roamed along, he sang a song, of the land of milk and honey,
Where a bum can stay, for many a day, and he don't need any
money.

Oh, the buzzin' of the bees, in the cigarette trees, by the soda water
fountain,
And the lemonade springs, where the bluebird sings,
In the Big Rock Candy Mountain.

In the Big Rock Candy Mountain, all the cops got wooden legs,
And the bulldogs all got rubber teeth,
And the hens lay soft- boiled eggs.

In the Big Rock Candy Mountain, you never change your socks,
And little streams of alcohol, come a-tricklin' down the rocks,

There's a lake of stew,
One of whiskey, too,
You can paddle around them in your own canoe,
In the Big Rock Candy Mountain.

"I'll be goddamned," exclaimed Billy one evening, "if you sorry
bunch of snot-nosed snipper-whappers and ten-thumbed tanglefooted
jackasses aren't almost getting the hang of it. If you keep it up, we might
even finish this summer, which would be good for you poor bastards,
because then you wouldn't have to come back and wrassle with me next
summer again. But don't get to thinking you might know what you are
doing. Wait till we get to the rockface ahead. That'll surely separate the

men from the boys, and there ain't but one man around here, and that's me."

The launch ride across the lake early each morning was full of cold shivers, each of us in light work shirts against the coming heat of the day. Packed in the boat with our gear, I once thought about a younger Billy Jiggs in the landing craft headed for that Normandy beach. He usually said very little, and never anything with his characteristic bombast, on those short trips across Jenny Lake, and I wondered if he was sometimes thinking the same thing.

The ride back in the evening, after the whoop and holler down the hillside, was very different. Warm from the day's work and the day's sun, hungry for Mrs. Green's inexhaustible dinners, spray from the cold bow-wave splishing over us, it was all jokes and laughter, highly obscene. Some days, as is common in the summer Rockies, there would be a short, sharp, hard thunderstorm at afternoon's end, drenching us as we crossed the lake. And, somehow, that could be best of all, as long as you didn't think excessively about being out in the middle of a lake, in a metal boat with metal tools, in a lightning storm, and with dynamite in the boat.

Each day, Billy made us carry the generator, the gas can, and the rock drill up the ever-lengthening distance to the end-of-trail. We left the sticks of dynamite in the boat, under cover, to be gone back for if needed. Most days we didn't blast on this section. Some days we would drill a couple of strategically-placed holes and then use a sixteen pound sledge to hammer off a protruding corner of a boulder that narrowed the trail. But some days we needed to blast.

Billy would mark out the places where rock needed to be blasted on the next day's section of the trail. During the following morning, with one or two of us helping him, he would fire up the drill from the generator and drill holes just where he wanted them, just as deep as he wanted them into the rock. I tried all summer to understand his calculus, and never could. But he was able, unerringly, to plan where to put the dynamite, how much, and at what angles to blow off just as much rock as he wanted out of the way.

After lunch break, he would stride, silent for once, up and down that stretch of tomorrow's trail, measuring and figuring by eye to judge if he had it just the way he wanted it. Any necessary corrections were drilled in. Then one of us, usually the one in the deepest doghouse that day, would be sent to run back down the trail to fetch a given number of sticks of dynamite and primer cord.

Work was ended a bit early on a blasting day, and all the crew except for the two who were chosen to act as Billy's blasting helpers were sent back to the boat. Most were able to do the whoop and holler, but at least one had to walk the backtrail to the lake, to make sure no bumbling tourist would wander up the wrong trail and get sent to heaven for his pains. Actually, we had blocked the old and new trail junction with stones and logs, and, that entire summer, we had no tourists stumble onto our work.

When the crew reached the boat below us, there was a loudly-hailed and echoed interchange of more-or-less formal signals, usually something like this.

"Hey, Billy, we're here and you ain't."

"Well, have you stumble-asses finally strolled your way down to where you can goof off for the next thirty minutes, not that you haven't been doing it all day?"

"Yeah, we're here, Billy. Don't blow your ass off, now. We'd miss you, and you'd miss it."

"Okay, I'm going to set her up, and give you a shout just before we blow. And whoever said that last remark is carrying the drill up tomorrow. And watch your heads and your tails, because I'm going to shoot them rocks right over you into the lake if I'm not careful, and Mrs. Jiggs says I'm never careful."

Then we would put the sticks of dynamite into the drilled holes, fuse end facing out, and Billy would attach the line of primer cord. He would carefully check the architecture and the arrangements once more, then run the cord a good distance around a corner or behind a big tree for safety, and, finally, attach it to the detonating electrical device (which, for some reason, we didn't carry up and down the hill each day, but left, wrapped in oilskin, up on the trail).

Then he would send his two helpers back down the trail a ways (not the hill, the trail) to safety, and have his last signals with those below.

"Are you ready for the Fourth of July, you pissants? Everybody safe?"

"Ready, Billy, give us a good one, now."

"Drop your cocks, drag up your socks, and get your heads down, boys. Here she goes.

FIRE IN THE HOLE!"

He would push the plunger down, making the electrical connection, and BAM, BAM, BAM. The line of charges would go off, rocks and splinters would fly everywhere, things would shoot up into the sky, pieces of hard sharp stuff would come clattering down onto the slope below. Sometimes even Billy didn't get it perfect, and rock would fly all the way out and down into the lake water, and Billy would run like hell down the slope (no whooping and hollering) to make sure his boys were all right. When she blew, we could hear from afar Billy's most joyous profanity, and could sometimes see him dancing a jig up on the trail. There is something at heart in all boys (whatever their age) that loves to blow things up, and the exhilaration of each day's blasting infected us all.

"Did you see that sumbitch fly? I swear it landed in the water not forty feet from us."

"Man, there was a piece as big as a stove come rolling down the hill like an express train!"

And so on.

After the festivities cooled down (and waiting a few moments to be sure there were no unexploded sticks just holding off to give you a nasty surprise), Billy called his two helpers back up the trail. They lugged down the generator, while Billy shouldered the drill, took the gas can in his other hand, and, just like Snow White and the Seven Dwarves, off went the jolly crew, home to dinner.

The debris was waiting for us, next morning, to shovel and lever out of the way, and then to get on with that day's section of trail.

Let me jump ahead of the story a little bit, because it was on this same section of the trail, about ten days later, where our conversation occurred with Mamma Bear and Baby Bear. It happened this way.

It was the usual beautiful morning, and we were walking up the trail to work, carrying our usual loads. Billy was off ahead, wanting to get up ahead of us to the work site (as usual) so he could spur us on with some choice sermon or other. A couple of the guys were behind him a ways, carrying tools. Then there was a gap, because the two boys carrying the heavy, and awkward, generator were having a hard time this morning, probably following a hard night. Then, a bit behind them, came me, humping the drill as penance for some infraction or other, and then the rest of the crew.

All of a sudden it got very quiet up ahead, with a total absence of the usual banter and chatter. Then the air was split by a low, prolonged, and I-mean-business growl. I stopped dead in my tracks, not sure whether to run forwards or backwards. The growl was repeated. I inched forward around a slight curve, and there they were.

Furthest up the trail was a big Mamma Bear, and she was not happy. In the middle were two petrified boys, each holding up one end of the heavy generator. Closest to me, up in a lodgepole pine, was Baby Bear, this year's cub, and he was calling for his Mamma.

She must have been up the hillside a ways from the trail, foraging for food, and left Baby in the tree for safety. Then along came the trail crew, and here we had it, a Teton Mountains Mexican Stand-off.

There are no grizzlys left in the Tetons, only black and brown bears (which are just different colors of the same species, and which should not be confused with the gigantic Alaskan browns and Kodiaks). They rarely give trouble to humans, except for causing nuisances around unattended camps and garbage dumps, or except if they get too used to humans feeding them, or except if they just take a mind to. However, there is a cardinal rule that says, "Never get between a sow and her cub." And that's where we, or more accurately, these two boys, were.

For a minute, nobody knew what to do. As for me, I was trying to think of which would be worse: have the bear come at me while I was burdened with the rock drill, or drop the drill and face Pappa Billy Bear's wrath later.

The boys then did exactly the right thing. They gently set the generator down in the middle of the trail, made quiet conversation noises, avoided eye contact with Mamma, did not look in Baby's direction, and backed slowly off the trail downhill from the bear (aggressive predators always try to get above their prey).

Mamma chuffed, whoofed, and snorted, ran back down the trail to the tree; the cub jumped down, and they both vanished into the forest above the trail, Mamma bringing up the rear and giving us the evil eye over her turned shoulder as she lumbered slowly into the trees.

When we all caught up with Billy at the end-of-trail, and told him what had happened, he said, "I doubt you were in any danger. What would a bear want with a gasoline generator, anyway?"

But let me tell you, for the next few days, when we walked that trail in the shadows of early morning or late afternoon, there was a lot of over-the-shoulder looking going on.

—▬▬—

By that first Tuesday, I was of course thinking of the coming Wednesday evening, with visions of Sarah's sugarplums dancing in my head. Jim and I had planned to go on up to the Jackson Lake Lodge, whether Dick turned up or not. But, as we reached the parked truck on the east side of Jenny Lake at the end of Wednesday's work, there was Dick, sitting on the ground and leaning back against one of the big tires. He had hiked out Cascade Canyon as planned, and was ready to hitch a ride back to park headquarters with us. This was the first of many occasions when I experienced a habit of Dick's that was characteristically reminiscent of the Mountain Men. He would casually mention that he would meet you at so-and-so place on such-or-such a day or time, and the rendezvous would be set for days or weeks away and miles and miles from where you were at the moment, often over rough country. And then he would just turn up, right on time and in place, as punctual as if he'd stepped off from the five twenty- three local from Grand Central Station.

We showered, shaved, slicked down (or up) what little hair we had on our heads, put on the cleanest clothes we had, did passable justice to Mrs. Green's six courses, and fired up Jim's Ford.

It was about quarter to seven when we got to the lodge, and we headed for the long rectangular recreation hall, surrounded by the one-story dorms. There was still plenty of light, and we three sat on the log rail fence for a few minutes before going into the rec hall.

Just above the eastern horizon, the beautiful blue-white Vega was rising, climbing slowly into the purpling sky to form the Summer Triangle with Altair of Eagle, and Deneb of Swan.

It became my habit that summer to always try and see Vega as night came on. To me she is among the most lovely of stars, fifth-brightest in the sky, Queen of Lyra. I am told that, in less than fifteen thousand years, Vega will be our Pole Star. I hoped, that June night in 1957, that on some evening, far, far into the future, some young man would sit, with the Tetons and Jackson Lake on his left hand, and Vega pointing the way to true north. And where would he be traveling?

At this early hour, the rec hall was not crowded. There was some music playing on forty-five rpm discs on a record player, nobody dancing, individuals scattered around game tables and relaxing on couches.

Kitty looked up from the Chinese Checkers game she was playing as we walked in, smiled, stood up, and walked directly over to Dick. She was tall (about three inches taller than Dick), lean and angular, almost, but not quite, to the point of bonyness, with long arms, legs that went all the way up, and slender elongated fingers. Brown hair, green eyes with little almost-orange flecks in them, and a smile that danced gently with her eyes. It was several evenings before I was absolutely sure I had heard her voice, in part because she spoke so quietly, and in part because she and Dick were usually off somewhere else before you knew it. When you watched her walk away with him, you could not be sure that her feet were actually touching the floor. Kitty could laugh and joke whole-heartedly, but even when she did, there was an air of serenity about her.

I realized that Dick was well accounted for, and indeed we did not see him again until the end of that evening. Jim, Dick, and I had arranged to meet at the Ford at ten o'clock, "just in case anybody got lucky." At the appointed time, I collected Jim from inside the rec hall, and, with Dick nowhere to be seen, we walked to the Ford. There, of course, was Dick, leaning against a fender.

I spotted Sarah sitting with a small group in a corner, so I wandered over and joined a conversation that soon worked its way into a twosome.

We traded basic biographies. Sarah was from a Mormon family over in Pocatello, Idaho: mom and dad, four brothers and sisters, dog and cat. She would be finishing up junior college this next year, and hadn't thought much about what came after that. Hadn't been much further east or west, except to Seattle one time, on her high school senior trip. Conversation sort of stopped there, except when we talked about the here and now, and the spell of these mountains. She was, with her straw-blonde hair and lake-blue eyes, limber figure, and sweet shy smile, as close to beautiful as I had seen, and she seemed clearly not reluctant to get to know me much, much better.

I was thinking about how best, and most rapidly, to make that possible, when a distraction intervened.

"Who, or what, is that?" I asked Sarah, as a tall but bulbous figure came through the door.

"That, or It, is Winston Carp, but you'd better call him Duke," she replied, suppressing a grin.

The Duke, as he insisted on being addressed, was an old guy, easily forty. He wore dress Western pants, brown tooled cowboy boots, a buckskin fringed jacket, a pearl-grey Stetson, and a fake rodeo belt buckle as big as a soup plate. Believe it or not, on his tooled belt was hung a Smith and Wesson thirty-eight "Chief"'s Special," with the four-inch barrel, and he had ByGod filled cartridge loops front and back on the belt. I guess that was in case five shots didn't do the job.

His face was pasty and somewhat bug-eyed, and his hands and feet were too big for their respective clothing cuffs. You never could see much of his hair, because it was always covered by the Stetson.

Here was his story: Duke was employed by the Lodge as sort of a night watchman, quasi-security guard. He interpreted this to mean that he was the Town Marshall, and he played this ridiculous role to the hilt. He would swagger in and out, making his rounds, hungry for attention but too maladroit to connect, particularly with the young girls he was most anxious to impress. As for the guys, he liked to give them the bad-eye stare, and it was all you could do to keep from saying to him, "Slap leather, partner." As one who myself had read too many Westerns, I *knew* that this guy had read *way too many* Westerns. But he was big, mean, and ugly, and everybody gave him plenty of room.

I looked over to see how Jim was doing. There he was, at a card table surrounded by six or eight pretty young things, all of whom were leaning closely around and into him. Do you remember those little toy Scotty dog magnets you used to get in the penny arcades, the ones where if you put the north pole of the black dog opposite the south pole of the white dog, they would clang together? Well, that was Jim with anything female within range. Jim was doing card tricks. These mostly involved, as nearly as I could tell, having one after another of the girls select a card, and place it back in the deck, which was then vigorously shuffled. Then Jim would reach out and, with a flourish and a snap of the pasteboard's corner, pluck the very same card from some barely-decent portion of the maiden's clothing or anatomy, to blushes, giggles, and hilarity on the part of all. No one, least of all Jim, seemed bored by the endless repetition of this maneuver, or the repartee by which he "explained" what he was doing. I could see that Jim was in good hands, or vice versa, and that I didn't have to worry about him for the rest of the evening.

Carp strolled menacingly around the hall, and stopped in front of Jim's table, leaning over a bit, probably to see if he could look down any of the girls' blouses in the process. With his thumbs in his belt, he addressed Jim.

"Well, another new smart aleck. You better watch your step, bud, I'll have my eye on you."

The room went silent. I moved up from where I was sitting, keeping my green Coke bottle in my hand. I figured Jim could spot Duke his seventy pounds of lard and still eat him for breakfast, but you never can be sure what's going to happen until it does.

Jim never even put down the card he had in his hand. He looked up, moved his chair back about six inches, smiled sweetly, and said, "Yessir, Mr. Marshall Wyatt Earp, Sir. I aim to be a peaceful citizen of Dodge"

All corners of the room erupted in laughter. Carp flushed a bright crimson, pulled down the tip of his Stetson with his left hand, ran his right hand over the right side of his belt, turned, and left the room with as much dignity as he could muster, doing a just-fair imitation of the cowboy-roll on the way.

I went back to the couch where Sarah sat, moved in a little closer, she moved in a little closer, and we both had the unusual idea of going outside for a little walk under the Wyoming stars.

We walked a bit, talked a (very little) bit, sat down under a tree, and softly began the process that was to occupy a good deal of my mental and physical energy for the next few weeks.

During those next two or three weeks, Sarah and I were going at it pretty hot and heavy. I would go up to the lodge every evening I could, with Jim in his Ford, or by my thumb, or Sarah would hitch down to Jenny Lake with some sandwiches cadged from the Jackson kitchen, and we would spend the evening on the shore of Jenny. The old round ridge in my wallet was long forgotten.

The rituals around the lodge were the eternal ones: young people beginning to pair off in the early summer. Often groups of us would take some beer, some ill-nourishing but tasty food, sleeping bags, and go off for a campfire evening near one of the lakes, or further up one of the canyons. We'd cook the hot dogs, drink the beer, talk in a circle, and then, letting the fire burn low, couples would snuggle down in the bags for several hours while the stars wheeled overhead.

Jim was almost always along, and almost always with a different partner, often with a girl none of us had seen before, a tourist passing through. Kitty would usually come, as one of a group who weren't paired off, unless we were going somewhere where Dick could walk out and meet us, which wasn't often.

But the fire also began to burn lower for Sarah and me. Perhaps it had been too much all at once. More likely, I thought, there just wasn't enough 'else' to keep the connection. By early July, we were seeing each other less and less often, and sometimes when I would get up to the lodge, I would not find her there, and be almost relieved. We would occasionally relight the flames, but it was clear to both of us that it was about over.

We were working hard now, Dick up in the Shining Mountains for most of the week, myself on the Hidden Falls Trail with Billy and the crew, and Jim driving his truck and providing far-flung counsel and comfort to female tourists. But for park summer employees, the weekends were made for adventure. Much of the time it was a males-only activity, since the waitresses and maids from the lodges worked a six-day week, and didn't always have a given Saturday or a Sunday off.

I would sometimes, when Kitty was not off on a weekend day, meet Dick at some point along one of the canyons, and we would hike for the day, coming out for a Saturday night at the lodge or in Jackson, or we would stay in the mountains and I would come out Sunday evening alone.

Sometimes we would fish over on the east side of the Hole, up in the Gros Ventre slide country (where, I think it was in the 1930s, a huge rock slide backed up the Gros Ventre river into a sizable lake), or further north, over by the Continental Divide. There was one lake, up fairly high, where we could usually count on pan-sized cut-throats with firm flesh the pink color of salmon. Even forty years later, I won't tell you the name of that lake. It's probably still there, if you want to go look for it.

Sometimes we would just horse around, as we had done on that first Sunday I was in the park, resting, larking, pseudo-fishing, and waiting for Saturday night to roll in.

And Dick and I began to fly.

It was true, as he had told me around a mouthful of pancake that first day, that he had his basic private pilot's license, and he was anxious to accumulate flying hours toward a commercial ticket. Jackson Hole had a small airport in those days. Dick had worked a deal with the manager of a small fleet, and for eighteen dollars an hour (including aviation fuel) he could rent a Cessna 172, one of the great single-engine workhorses, and we could take her anywhere we wanted. Nine dollars apiece was significant but not impossible money to us that summer. Dick would come out for Friday or Saturday evening, stay over in the bunkhouse, and we would hitch out to the airport north of Jackson early in the morning, and crank her up. As the Hole was warmed by the sun, the air would rise up the slopes of the Tetons, providing terrific thermals for bounce and lift, maybe a little dangerous along the mountain faces, especially in a single-engine job, but not to our young eyes. We would fly up and down the valley, getting as close in to the canyons and peaks as we dared, loving the bumps, but never flying across the tops. I say "we", but of course it was Dick who was doing the flying. I would sit in the shotgun seat, and from time to time he would let me have the stick—what a thrill those morning flights were!

When we could, which basically meant when Kitty was free, we would take girls up with us. The 172 was a four-seater, and that just worked fine.

The best trips of all were when we would fly up to, and around Yellowstone, which meant two hours of flight time. Have you ever seen a reproduction of Moran's masterpiece painting, "The Grand Canyon of the Yellowstone," which was hung in the US Capitol? Well, that is what the canyon looks like, a great deep cleft running straight up to the Yellowstone Falls at its head. We would fly up that canyon, as low to the rims on either side as Dick dared, and as close up to the falls as what little prudence we had allowed.

What we did in that Rocky Mountain airspace that summer, you could not do today, and there are plenty of good reasons why you shouldn't do it, then or now. But what a way to see those Shining Mountains! Sometimes I would look out over the side as we skimmed the forested lower slopes, and persuade myself that, far below, I could see a short pack train—Jedediah and Davy mounted up, with a couple of mules on long leads carrying their traps and gear, moving along slowly in their buckskins, beaded moccasins, and fur caps with a bluejay or magpie feather stuck in them, up and into their mountains. Davy would look up, his face shining in the sun, and give a wave, or lift the long rifle from the crook of his left arm and raise it up over his head. When I told Dick about it, he said, "Well, might as well wave back, then." And he would waggle the wings of the Cessna in salute.

So the summer blossomed toward fullness. The days were warmer now, the nights still cool or even cold. By now even the hardest of the day's work felt pleasurable instead of painful. The darker, wilder nights were yet to come; the evenings still possessed a kind of innocence. As Sarah and I drifted apart, neither with regrets, I felt a vague unease. What I wanted, of course, was Kitty.

— ANOTHER BEAR, AND TROUBLE ALL AROUND —

What was it about Kitty? By conventional standards, certainly by the standards of the Fifties—putting a premium on lots of hair and lots of bust, tail, and thigh—she wasn't beautiful, good-looking, or even "pretty." Modigliani might have posed her as a model, but she wasn't severe; the angular planes of her face and body had a softness, almost a blurred quality, to their edges. Her movements, like her voice, whispered rather than shouted. If Kitty had been a young tree, she would have been a mountain aspen.

As Sarah and I cooled down, I began to spend most of my 'lodge time' in Kitty's company. She and Dick were firmly paired. Dick was hardly around at all during the week, I was Dick's good friend, and so I became Kitty's as well. This was, on my part, more than a little hormonally uncomfortable. I was fully aware of how attracted I was to her, not attraction really, more like somewhere in between obsession and infatuation, and nearer to the latter.

We passed many evening hours just talking together, or sitting around the rec hall with others, playing cards, horsing around, just spending easy time. You could say that she was waiting for Dick, and I was waiting for her.

Was Kitty aware of the ambivalence I felt in our situation? If so, she never let on. And the more time we spent together, the better I got to know her gentle nature, and the more I wanted her.

— ◆ —

By now we were well into the month of July, and, up on the trail, we were at the edge of the rockface, which was really more likely an old rock slide. It was steep, and littered with boulders, many of which were too huge and too deeply buried into the face, to move out of the way by hand. A large area of shale and scree, above and below the line of trail, made it impractical to go around. There were almost no trees, which meant that there was very little good moist brown dirt, mostly just sandy scraps between and under the rock.

No trees also meant no shade, except for what you could get in the shadows of the largest boulders. We were well over halfway between the lake and Hidden Falls, so that meant a long walk for water if we used up what we had. And with much more drilling for blasting, we also needed water to cool the drill bit as it tore into hard rock. No shade meant less-comfortable smoke-and lunch-breaks, unless we wanted to walk up or back down the trail into the cool of the shaded forest, which we almost always did.

The scree and the uneven rocky terrain meant that footing was less certain, and purchase for hard swinging of shovel, hammer, pick, prybar, or sledge less effective. Dust and gritty earth thrown into our faces from the work meant more discomfort and more thirst, which meant more depletion of our waterbags, which meant heavier loads or more trips back down to the lake.

I am sure that the passage across the rockface was really not longer in distance than several hundred yards. But in my July dreams, and in the dreams of the many years since then, it extended for uncounted miles, hard work with no interim areas of respite, each stage of building every yard, and then finishing out the details of every yard, a challenge to the crew's physical and mental toughness.

I think I learned as much about myself over those few hundred yards of rock, or those dream miles, as over any comparable distance I have traveled in my life.

Strangely enough, we loved it. The crew worked together there better than anywhere else on that trail. You could hear the tools come down harder, and with more resolution in the swing. At the end of breaks (and that sure was good advice I had gotten on the very first day about hopping right to it when Billy blew the back-to-work whistle), you could see the determination in our eyes to strike harder, last longer, cut cleaner.

And I noticed something about Billy that I hadn't previously. The harder the work was, the easier (and quieter) he was on us. On the rock-face, we almost came to regret the decrease of his cussing us and poking pseudo-scorn at our efforts. Besides, not one of us worked harder than Billy did.

Whether it was deliberate or not, I am not certain, but the songs changed character as we moved deeper onto the face. Chain-gang songs, outlaw songs, "Midnight Special" down-in-prison songs.

Take this hammer (hunh), carry it to the Captain.
Take this hammer (hunh), carry it to the Captain.
Take this ham-mer, carry it to the Captain,
Tell him I'm gone, tell him I'm gone.

If he asks you (hunh), was I runnin'.
If he asks you (hunh), was I runnin'.
And if he asks you, was I runnin',
Tell him I was flyin', tell him I was flyin'.

This old chain gang (hunh), cain't hold me, boys.
This old chain gang (hunh), cain't hold me, boys.
This old cha-ain gang, cain't hold me, boys,
Flyin' up to Heaven, I'm flyin' up to Heaven.

John Hardy was a desperate little man,
He carried a pistol every day.
Killed him a man in the West Virginia land,
Oughta' see John Hardy get away, boys,
Oughta' see Johnny Hardy get away.

John Hardy ran over the East Stone Bridge,
Thinking that he would go free.
Up stepped the sheriff with his boys in blue,
Said, Johnny, now, why don't you come with me,
Johnny, now, why don't you come with me.

I been to the East, and I been to the West,
I been this whole world round.
I been to the river, and I been baptised,
I'm ready for my hole in the ground.
Yes, I'm ready for my hole in the ground.

I could feel the hardness of the days become reflected in the hardness of my arm, and of my leg, my muscles absorbing and storing the heat and energy of the mountain sunshine. When we got up on the trail in the morning, we would first shovel, scrape, and lever away the debris of the previous afternoon's blasting. Some of it we could throw over the side, rolling it down the hill, or using it for building up the outside edge of the trail. Some of it we could use to level out and fill in the way itself. Almost always we had to go back down into the forest to dig up earth to use to create and cover the smooth surface of the trail, and that meant our bringing a wheelbarrow up, which, blessedly, Billy didn't make us carry down each night. As Rod said to him, reflecting Billy's own earlier words, "Why would a bear want a wheelbarrow, anyway?"

While that was going on, several of us would help Billy lay out the line for the next day, and start the drilling. As that was underway, others would begin to cut and build what trail we could, skipping around the parts to be drilled and blasted. If you think about it, that left a lot of short lines that had to match up end to end. Billy was death on any that didn't, or that required a curve to make them fit.

By late afternoon, the process of setting up that day's section, and clearing out that of the day before, was complete ("Or it better-by-God-had-fire-and-damnation-to-hell-be," said you-know-who), and we could get going with the blasting as earlier described.

I grew to dearly love the drilling and blasting process, vying with the others to be chosen to assist Billy with both on as many days as possible. Holding that heavy, perpendicular, bucking, drill against the rock at the right angle, feeling the strain and vibration across your belly and up through your arms into your chest, watching the water spray back at you as it was poured by your buddy onto the junction of drill and stone, hearing Billy shout, "That's deep enough, you brainless bastard, are you planning to drill all the way through to Idaho?"—it may be trite to say, but you got the feeling that you were really doing something.

And then setting the charges, and blowing that rock sky-high—you *really* got the feeling that you were really doing something. As Paul said to me in the launch crossing Jenny Lake one evening,"WHAM, BAM, SLAM, KABLAM—SHAZZAM, CAPTAIN MARVEL! Is there anything better you can do standing up with your clothes on?"

One thing, though. When you start working with dynamite, just being around and handling that TNT can give you a pounding head-ache, especially if you are working and sweating hard. You absorb it through your skin. I would go back to the bunkhouse in the evening with the vessels in my brain so dilated my hat size felt like it must have been several numbers higher. Dynamite migraine is what that is, caused by the same mechanism as putting nitroglycerine tablets under your tongue to open up your cardiac vessels, when you get a few decades older than we were then. I never got used to it all summer. But, and here is a lesson you can apply to better understanding the behavior of your young grandsons: "drilling them in, lighting them off, and watching them fly, is worth the punishment, fifty times over."

I also began to spend more evenings with Jim, and most of those evenings were down in the town of Jackson. When he was up in the park in the evening, Jim usually had other, sweeter, fish to fry than sitting around playing Chinese Checkers or Monopoly in the rec hall. Talk about a girl in every port: that old black Ford could be found in Colter Bay, Signal Mountain, Jenny Lake, and most points in between. Sometimes he would ask me along, but mostly he was a man on a solo mission, doing his duty to spread joy and light, and probably some pollen as well, wherever he was needed.

But I noticed that, more and more often, he would head toward town after dinner in the bunkhouse, and so I wasn't completely surprised when, one evening before mealtime, he said, "Steve, why don't you come into town with me to eat tonight. There's somebody I 'd like you to meet."

"Well, if she can cook like, but doesn't look like, Mrs Green, I'll give it a try," I replied, and Jim just grinned. "You'll eat those words, you sarcastic bugger."

We left the Ford on one of the streets surrounding the city park, walked diagonally through the park, and headed for the bakery on one of the northeast side streets. Jim explained that they served good food as well, "especially the pork chops."

"Steve, I'd like you to meet Petey. Petey, this is a bad man, but he's hungry."

She was slim as a deer, and twice as graceful. Black straight hair hung halfway down her back. Her eyes were obsidian black, set in a face two shades short of copper. Her smile was both shy and challenging at the same time. You could see in her the traces of her Shoshone grand-mother. That grandmother must have been herself the great-great-great-grand daughter of a young girl who was there on that day in 1805 when Lewis and Clark made the first American contact with Sacagawea's people. The Shosone would trade them the horses that would make it possible for the Corps of Discovery to cross the Bitterroot Mountains, just a few hundred miles from where we now stood, in a bakery in Jackson, Wyo-ming, one hundred and fifty-one years and eleven months and some days later. And we were in the company of a lithe young beauty in slim-hipped jeans, low-heeled, narrow-toed Roper boots, a yoked purple Western shirt with pearl buttons, a white apron that had stenciled on it, "Let 'er Buck!", and a flour-dusted nose.

"Hi, Petey, Jim's been telling me how much he loves your pork chops."

We ate well that evening: pork chops, fresh vegetables, apple sauce, cowboy coffee, and as many doughnuts as can fit inside two hungry young men.

"You know, Steve, I'm working up a plan I'd like to talk with you about, but I haven't quite got it all figured out yet."

It occurred to me that any plan Jim worked up would have a good chance of getting us rich, famous, in jail, or any combination of the above, but would undoubtedly entail having a hell of a lot of fun in the process, so I held my peace until the scheme should ripen. We didn't have a chance to talk about it further for some days, as that evening we sat until past closing time in the bakery, helping Petey get rid of the un-sold, day-old stock, laughing, and talking. It was obvious that Jim was smitten. In his own way, of course.

So I began to spend more nights down in Jackson, with Jim. That meant that most nights I would end up hitching back to Moose on my lonesome, as Jim would stay down later with Petey, coming back to the bunkhouse past midnight or not at all.

While waiting for Petey to finish up at the bakery, Jim and I began to frequent the Horseman.

The little town of Jackson must have had more than half a dozen bars (a few years earlier, one would have called them saloons) on its main street in those days, and the Horseman was the biggest, and, we thought, the best. It sat right on a corner of the main street, across from the southwest corner of the city park. It was a false-fronted, big, single-roomed place, all in wood and log trim, the outside and inside logs peeled, and shiny with clear varnish. There was, of course, a long bar across one side, tables and chairs scattered across the floor, a small bandstand at the back where local groups played on the weekend. It was well-lit, with a huge front window facing the park. Above the bar hung what was for those days a big-screen TV (probably replacing within the past five years the formerly obligatory portrait of the buxom reclining nude).

The crowd was a mix of tourists and locals (and I wasn't quite sure where Jim and I fit into that division). It was a good-natured place in a good-natured time, and there was rarely trouble, at least inside the establishment. One evening I did see an Idaho cowboy, somewhat the worse for wear, ride his pony up the boardwalk, through the swinging doors, and, belly and saddle, right up to the bar. The bartender threw the horse out, but let the cowboy stay. It would have made a better story, and delighted the crowd, had he done the opposite—gotten rid of the cowboy but kept the pony, but that's not the way it happened, at least not that night.

The black and white television was usually tuned to sports, and especially to the fights. Jim and I discovered that we had both boxed in college, and had also both had a little street experience, so we liked to be there on the nights (I think it was Fridays) when there was nationally-televised boxing. That year, there were two young fighters of special interest. One was a wild light-heavyweight named Hurricane Jackson, who would, without much style but plenty of energy, overwhelm his opponents with flurries of windmill punches. I doubt that few people reading this remember him today. The other, a lean and hungry and oh-so-classy young tiger, who had just turned pro after winning Olympic gold, was named Cassius Clay. Once you had seen him, you would never forget him.

So we spent more evenings in Jackson, ate at the bakery, drank at the Horseman, and I put on more thumb miles getting back to Moose. And one Friday in late July, Jim said to me," I've about got 'er worked out. Let's talk about it next week."

On a Thursday in late July, I had a telephone message awaiting me at park headquarters when we got in from work. It was from Kitty: " Dick sent me out a message by one of the guys coming down from the mountains that he couldn't make it out of the canyon this weekend, but that, if I could get up there, we could spend some time together on Sunday. I have the day off, and Dick says you know where their trail camp is. Steve, could you go up with me?"

Well, of course I could, and would. I knew the camp location and the canyon. I was in love with the mountains, and more than half in love with the lady. I only told her the first part, and we agreed that we would meet, early Sunday morning, at the Jenny Lake lodge.

Dick's crew were working up in Leigh Canyon, the most northerly-but-one canyon in the heart of the park. It runs into Leigh Lake, after passing along the flank of the awesome ramparts and glaciers guarding the southern aspect of Mount Moran. Leigh is a relatively narrow, steep-walled canyon, with its creek running down the middle. The trail up the canyon was rather primitive, and Dick and Company were working far up the canyon, looking for trail repairs or blockages that had to be seen to. There is an un-named small lake about two miles from the canyon mouth, and another, Mink Lake, a further four miles up from that; the camp should lie somewhere between the two.

Kitty and I met in the cool of early morning, about eight o'clock, at Jenny Lake Lodge, the day starting with the usual near-cloudless blue sky. Just another ho-hum day in Paradise. We had a long day ahead of us: about three and a half miles from the lodge to the canyon mouth, and then anywhere from three to five miles up the slope of the canyon. With the return trip, that would make at least fifteen miles, say eight hours walk give or take a bit. Allowing for spending two or three hours up there with Dick, that came to nearly twelve hours, with a safety factor built in. That Teton arithmetic meant that we should be back at Jenny at the latest around eight pm, with still a little twilight left, and plenty early enough to pick up a Sunday night hitch back to Jackson Lake Lodge. We had plenty of cold water in the creek, some trail snacks, flashlights, and light jackets in a small pack, but no raingear.

The hike up was wonderful. Neither of us was inclined to push it, though I knew Kitty was eager to reach Dick. I'd lead for a while, and then we would switch. I liked that even better, watching her slim body and firm behind on the trail ahead of me. We passed a moose working the shallows where Leigh Lake comes into String Lake, we saw and heard lots of birds in the mouth of the canyon, and, when we stopped to rest and snack, the noisy Whiskey Jacks would come around for hand-outs, actually hopping up onto our knees where we had placed tidbits, the greedy devils.

We passed no-name lake, we moved through a beautiful broader area of the canyon, but we saw no trace of a camp. We started the steeper climb up to Mink Lake, knowing that the camp had to be there, where there was plenty of water, and flatter ground.

Well, the camp was there, but there was nobody in it, and no message left as to where they had gone. I could see a mixture of disappointment and irritation in Kitty's face.

And then we looked more closely, and saw that the deserted camp was the least of anybody's problems. There had been a visitor before us, and Brother Bear had really done a job on that campsite.

One tent, probably the one that had held supplies, had been slashed and shredded. The remnants of a sleeping bag's innards were strewn about the ground. Cans and boxes lay everywhere, usually at some distance from their scattered former contents. Of most impressive note, a small metal ice-box had been squeezed by main force into an irregular diamond shape—with the door closed.

"Steve, maybe they were here when the bear came in, and maybe one of them is hurt, and that's why they're not in camp."

"I doubt it, Kitty, because if there had been real trouble, and surely if anyone was hurt, they would have had to come out by the trail, passing us as we came up, and we know they didn't do that. No, I think that this bear came in and raised hell with the camp empty. Look, their meat and most of their food is still hanging up from that high tree branch. Odds are that they took off somewhere for the day, maybe just exploring up to Cirque Lake high up there to the north, nothing much else scheduled to do (oops, wrong thing to say to Kitty), and the bear came in after they had left."

Well, we shouted and whistled some, at the mountains, which of course was of no use. We cleaned up the camp as best we could. We decided to wait at least three hours, just in case there was someone in need of help. And we sat there, with not much scintillating conversation. I passed the time thinking of lots of wonderful ways to spend three hours with Kitty, but nothing that went on that day was any of them. Kitty was pretty steamed, and spent a good deal of the time thinking aloud about what she was going to put in the note to Dick that we would leave at the campsite before we started down. On the theory that gentlemen don't read one another's mail, I never looked at the note, but I bet it seared his ears. And he deserved it, my friend, the thoughtless bastard.

We hung around the trail camp site until too late in the afternoon, the way you often will when you are not really sure you want to start down a long trail. It was well after four, without any sign of Dick or the crew, when I noticed that thunderheads were gathering over the peaks northwest of us.

"Kitty, we better get a move on. Even if they show up now, we would have to get started pronto. It looks like some weather might be moving in."

"Ok, dammit (Kitty was not above using strong language when the occasion warranted), let me just leave Dick this note, and then let's get to it."

We started down, and were past the steeper descent and into the more open part of the canyon when we heard the first cannoncracks of thunder over the peaks, and saw the purple-black clouds begin to roll towards us. The wind came up rapidly, and then, as is often the pattern in the Rockies, the hard rain was preceded by even-harder hail.

The hailstones weren't very big, less than thumbnail-size, but they stung, especially since neither of us had a hat or rain gear. We got in under some trees, and thus lost more time. Most of the lightning was concentrated up high over the peaks, and we felt fairly safe in the canyon. When the rain began, we moved on, but picking our way more slowly now, and we became thoroughly soaked and chilled-through during the hour-long rainstorm.

By the time the rain stopped, the afternoon shadows had darkened the narrow canyon, and we had no chance to get warm and dry in sunshine.

So we walked out of Leigh Canyon, wet, cold, hungry, discouraged, and late. It was almost nine-thirty by the time we crossed the String Lake footbridge, and we still had about two miles to go to reach the North Jenny Lake Junction, where we could pick up the main park road, and, hopefully, a hitch. We thought briefly about heading down to the Jenny Lake Lodge, but that small and refined place would be pretty well rolled up and snoring by this hour, and anyway Kitty had to be on duty at six-thirty Monday morning, which would make getting a ride up to the Jackson Lake Lodge at five-thirty very problematic. We decided to push on.

By the time we reached the junction, we knew we had made a mistake. It was after ten o'clock on a Sunday night, after a heavy storm, and there was no traffic on the road. We stood on the edge of the asphalt for twenty minutes or so, both of us dog-tired, and then I realized Kitty was shivering. In truth, I didn't feel so chipper myself.

"Kitty, let's move back into the trees, try to get warm, and rest. If a car comes along, we'll hear it in plenty of time to run out to the road. The woods are wet, but we can probably make a fire if we have to. We need to get warm, Kitty."

We moved back into the forest twenty yards or so, and I settled back against a big pine. Kitty sat, curled between my spread knees, and leaning back against my chest. I took off my jacket, put my arms around her, and spread the jacket as best I could over the front of us both. She shivered for a few minutes (which, though it is not very chivalrous of me to admit, I found incredibly erotic), and then began to relax, breathe softly and regularly, and was soon asleep. I tried to keep my eyes open, but dozed off, feeling her hair move gently as I breathed against it.

We had been sleeping together (if you can call it that) for about a half-hour, when I heard the sound of a motor coming north on the road. I shook Kitty awake, and we dragged ourselves out from the trees, thumbs held up.

It was two whiskey'd guys in an old Dodge pickup, and even by the rising moon you could see it was held together mainly by rust and paint. But it looked awfully good, they stopped, we squeezed all four of us into the cab, and we were at the foot of the hill to the lodge in less than twenty minutes.

There was no chance of my getting a ride back down to Moose at that hour. Kitty suggested that she check with whoever she could find in the guys' dorm, and try to locate me an empty bunk or a place on the floor there. The rec hall was shut and locked, so the dorm seemed the best available alternative. Within minutes she was back with a boy I knew slightly, and within minutes after that I was snoring, fully clothed, on an empty cot, boots on and a blanket draped over me.

———

"Where is he? I'll skin the bastard when I find him. Open up all the room doors and let me have a look." The voice and the manner were unmistakable: Duke.

My roommate slipped back in through the door. "You had better hustle out of here. Duke has gone nuts, has his gun out, and is looking for some intruder. It's seven in the morning, and I don't know how he knows you're here, but you'd better hop it."

Since I already had my boots on, all I had to do was throw off the blanket, slide back a window, peek out to be sure the coast was clear, and, levering myself out to the ground, scuttle down between the buildings and away. My brain was still foggy, and I couldn't make out what the big deal was, but I was awake enough to know that Duke might just be crazy enough to start shooting if he saw me. I guess this was the Town Marshall's big chance.

I made it uneventfully down to the road, and once again stuck out my thumb. It was too late to get back to the Moose bunkhouse for cleanup and breakfast, so my plan was to ride down only to Jenny Lake, and meet the crew there. What a nice surprise for them!

A ride appeared in short order. I was there at the boat dock when Billy and the crew arrived. From their expressions, I suppose that I looked pretty much like a guy who had been up in the mountains, rained and hailed on, slept in the woods, chased out a window by a madman with a pistol, and had missed dinner and breakfast to boot.

Billy didn't say a word, just gave me a funny look, and, of course, selected me to carry the drill up the trail.

Mondays at work can be (pardon the choice of words) a bear, and this one was that in spades. I managed to get through it, the boys covered for me bit, and they scavenged a lunch for me between all the sacks. Billy gave me half his apple.

At day's end, we were gathering up our tools, and I just knew Billy was about to invite me to carry the drill back down the hill, when a sonorous voice, further magnified through a battery-powered megaphone, echoed up the hill from the lakeshore.

"Steve Jonas, if you are up there, come down immediately. Do you hear me, come down immediately. Steve Jonas, do you hear me?"

I looked at Billy, he looked at me, and just gave a jerk of his head. I raced down the slope to the lake.

My first thought was that there was some family emergency back home. My second was that I was in some kind of deep trouble, but I couldn't think of what that would be.

At the lakeshore, I met Corey Green, standing, legs astride, belly somewhat precariously balanced, in a small boat with an outboard motor. "Get in the boat, son."

"What's happened, Corey, what's up?"

"Just get in the boat, son. We'll talk back at park headquarters." And he said not another word on the journey across the lake, and down the road in the pale green US Park Service pickup.

He preceded me into the administration building office, arranged his belly between his swivel chair and the desk, put his feet up on the desk, and motioned me into a chair facing him.

"I had a call from the Jackson Lake Lodge. They said there was an intruder in the dorms last night. They believe it was you. They want to charge you with breaking and entering, though I gather that nothing is missing. You're in trouble, son."

"Corey, that's a load of baloney. I didn't do anything wrong. Well, maybe I entered, but I didn't break. You know I'm not a criminal." And I told him the whole story, perhaps just taking a little bit off the part about holding Kitty in my arms in the woods.

" The Lodge says that if you will leave the area immediately and permanently, they won't press charges. Maybe that's the best idea, son."

"Corey, I 'm not leaving these mountains until the season's over. And I'm not leaving the crew, and I'm not leaving the trail, unless you fire me, and I don't want you to do that."

"Is that the truth, son?"

"Yes, it is, all of it."

"Well, I can probably handle them dude wranglers. But you better stay out of trouble, son."

"Thanks, Corey, you know I'm okay, and I'll watch myself."

"Alright, get out of here. And make sure my Ma gets you enough to eat tonight. You look like something the coyotes left behind. But you had better stay away from the lodge for a couple of days. That Duke Carp is a doofus, and he takes himself too seriously, but doofuses who take them-selves too seriously can be dangerous."

"Right. Thanks, Corey, I'm going right now. I'll watch it. And I'll eat a big dinner. And thanks."

And, as he usually did, he waited until I was almost out the door to fire his last shot.

"Oh, yeah, by the way, son, did you get laid?"

"What? No, Corey, at least not this time."

"Well, my advice is, if you're gonna get everybody steamed up like this, the next time you ought to bunk in the girl's dorm, get yourself a little piece, and at least get something out of it for all your trouble."

⁓ JACKSON'S BLACK HAT GANG ⁓

"**H**ere's the way it looks to me, Steve," Jim said to me, as we were sitting over a few beers in the Horseman, several evenings after my talk with Corey. I had stayed away from the lodge, had not seen nor talked with Kitty, and, given my reprieve, was trying as hard as possible to be the All American Trail Crew Poster Boy on the job. I was sure that the story, most likely garishly embellished in repeated tellings, of what had transpired up at the lodge that past Sunday night was all over the park, but I didn't talk much about it to Billy or the crew, thinking that the less said the better. Besides, any exaggerated rumors might actually make it look like I was more of a daredevil than was so, and no nineteen-year-old male can resist that opportunity.

"Here we are, spending most of our evenings in Jackson, you having to ride your thumb back to Moose if I stay over down here late with Petey," Jim continued."We have thirty-five bucks for room and board taken out of our checks, so in a sense we are paying double for all the meals we eat with Petey at the bakery. If we lived down here in Jackson, and I drove us back and forth from the park each work day, we could save that money, waste less time, and all around it would be more convenient."

"Hold on, pard," I replied. "It surely would be more convenient for you, and it might have some advantage for me, too, since I think I'll be spending a lot less time up at the lodge for the rest of the summer, but anyway you look at it, finding a place to live in Jackson has got to cost us a lot more than bunking up at Moose. As for hitching back up to the Park, I have to get up there anyway for round-up early in the morning."

"Got'cha, buddy." (as usual, Jim had all the details figured out in advance, and was carefully leading me down the garden path), "Just listen to the deal. I know this old guy here in town, in fact he's sort of an uncle of mine, but not really. He has some vacant space in his backyard that he will let us camp out in. Now, I've already talked with Buddy, the trail crew oversight chief, and there is some extra camping gear in storage up in the park: a tent, cots, tarp, etc, that he says nobody will mind if we liberate for a few weeks." (In fact, what Jim was probably saying was that nobody would *know* where the equipment was for a month or so.) "We can set up the tent in the back yard, and be sitting pretty. Eat at the bakery or wherever we want, Silver Dollar, Chuckwagon, be right here in town every night to do whatever we want, and save some of that thirty-five dollars per paycheck to spend right here in the Horseman. I'm pretty sure we can talk the park folks into letting us shower and such in the bunkhouse if we need to, and there we go."

As a Jim-scheme went, this one didn't sound too hare-brained. I was reasonably confident that he wouldn't actually expropriate the camping gear without some kind of authorization from Buddy, however informal, and the idea did make some sense. We were beginning to spend most of our evenings down in Jackson. This way we could grab breakfast in the bakery, which opened very early, take a light lunch with us, and eat dinner wherever we pleased. Obviously, Jim wanted lots more time with Petey, and I didn't mind helping him out with that. As to whether we would actually save any money or not, I wasn't sure Jim was right. Holding on to an extra dollar instead of having a good time with it right here and now was not that Nebraska cowboy's strongest suit. But, all together, it sounded like a pretty good idea, and worth a try.

When we told Corey and Mrs. Green that we were thinking of "moving out" and sleeping in a tent in town, their reaction was less than enthusiastic. I think Mrs. Green's twin worries were that we wouldn't get enough to eat, and that we would be corrupted by the fleshpots of Jackson. Corey wanted to be sure that we would get up to the park in time for work every morning, "after staying out and raising who knows what twelve kinds of Hell every night in town." When we explained to him, somewhat illogically, that we were doing that already anyway, and that it was only eleven kinds, he came around a bit. All in all, they were pretty good about it in the end. Mrs. Green whispered to me, when she thought Corey couldn't hear, "Now, of course you boys can use the bunkhouse to wash up in, whenever you want. And if you miss breakfast or something, I'm sure we'll be able to find you a few odds and ends to keep you going. You be careful, there, down in town every night with all those big-city tourists and such."

So we lugged that gear (under cover of dusk, it is true) down to Jackson, and set it up in old Mr. MacGregor's garden. He lived on the unfashionable south edge of town (in Jackson, in those days, the edge wasn't a far walk from the center), about three blocks from the Horseman, three blocks from the Silver Dollar, and five blocks from the bakery. What could be better than that? As near as I could tell, Mr. MacGregor didn't do much of anything all day, and so was happy to have us around, and more than glad when he could waylay us to chat and tell tall stories with for a few minutes in the morning, evening, or anytime, around a jug of his homemade dandelion wine or a six-pack of Coors. There was plenty of room in the straggly back yard, between the house and the shed, and there was even an outhouse for our convenience, and a water tap and garden hose for our personal hygiene. We had a groundcloth against the damp, a spacious fore-and-aft pole tent that kept most of the rain off, two comfortable cots for our sleeping bags, and a Coleman lantern or two.

Our clothes and other gear were either scattered in cardboard boxes (appropriated from the local market) around the tent, or in reserve in Jim's Ford. Not a bad arrangement, after we had it all in place.

Of course, there was one other angle that Jim had figured, and I hadn't. The tent gave him a place for some private time with Petey. We worked out a signal, so that when they didn't want to be disturbed, he would leave a lit Coleman lantern *outside* the tent flap. Given all the evening hours I spent roaming around waiting for that outside lantern to be extinguished, I got to know "Jackson by dark" pretty well, and could even have given walking tours to the tourists, had I been so inclined.

It also became apparent that there had begun an increasing number of errors in the park's bunkhouse kitchen. Almost every day, one of the Hidden Falls crew would find a duplicate apple or an extra sandwich in his lunch sack, and Billy almost always had an extra cookie or three to pass on to me.

─── ───

One Sunday, shortly after Jim and I had moved to Jackson, the two of us and Dick were headed up to Colter Bay, just to have a look around the north end of the park, and to see if there were any new girls working at the store and cabins there.

We stopped to have lunch at the Chuckwagon at Moose Junction, something we did not normally do, because, though the beef was great, the prices were strictly for the tourists. However, it was Sunday, the sun was shining, and Jim and I were mindful of all that money we were saving by living in the tent in Jackson. And, since the Chuckwagon was "all you can eat," served cowboy trail-camp style from the kettles and grills under the tent, we probably didn't come out too badly on the deal, especially counting the stuff we rolled up in napkins and kerchiefs to save for the evening meal to come.

Heading up the park road after lunch, as we passed the turn-off road to Lupine Meadows, at the south end of Jenny Lake, we saw a cluster of vehicles parked scattered on the verge of the road: Park Service pick-ups, Forest Ranger utilities, one or two private cars, and an ambulance. There was no sign of a road accident, so we figured someone must have gotten in trouble in the canyons or on the mountains, and stopped to see if we could help.

We were filled in by the Ranger who was overseeing the rescue. "Three climbers had a bad fall yesterday afternoon up on Teewinot. One was able to hike out to Jenny Lake Lodge last night and call for help. Buddy and the mountain rescue team have been up there since first light this morning, trying to get the other two down. One, I gather, is busted up pretty bad, and they both have been laying out all night on the mountain. They've got them almost off the mountain now, and we're trying to organize a chain of carriers for the litters, so stick around if you can."

Though the hardest and most delicate work would have been bringing the injured climbers off the mountain face, the carry off the lower slopes and across the mile or so of uneven ground, including a stretch of marshy area, would need lots of less-expert hands. Today, those climbers would probably have been lifted by helicopter straight off the mountain to the small hospital in Jackson, or flown on from Jackson for more intensive care at a medical center, but those services were not readily available back in the 1950s in northwestern Wyoming.

The three of us got up near the head of the line in the forest where the rescue team would come out, figuring we would walk alongside the first litter carriers until they needed to be spelled. Buddy and the four other rescue team members turned up shortly, Buddy carrying one of the injured, piggy-back style, with one of the climber's splinted legs sticking straight out. The other climber was supported in a two-man chair-carry between team members. Both were gaunt, dazed, and obviously suffering from exposure in addition to their injuries. The rescue team, for their part, also looked like they had been through the mill, hauling these guys down over steep and dangerous terrain, cross-country, from somewhere near the ten-and-a-half thousand foot level to where the litter bearers could start to relieve them at about three thousand feet lower down.

Four men to each of the two Stokes basket litters made short, but heavy, work of the last stretch. Everybody pitched in, and soon saw the two off for Jackson in the ambulance. I asked Buddy, who was gathering together the rescue gear, what had happened.

"Well, the three of them were up at about ten-six, working their way up above a little rocky cirque well below those glaciers between Mounts Owen and Teewinot. The lead guy, the one who was able to walk out after the accident, had one of his buddies roped-up on belay, and the third climber was free, below that. A little weather suddenly came in, with some hail. The top climber slipped, the belayer lost him, and as he went down, the one who was falling knocked the lower one off. The two of them fell and rolled only about twenty feet, give or take a little, but were banged up on the rocks. One guy looks like he might have a concussion or maybe a more severe head injury, and has a lot of facial lacerations and maybe a broken elbow. The guy who is badly hurt has at least a broken femur, and seems to me might have some internal injuries. The belay man got off with a bruised wrist and an ankle sprain, and just toughed it out to make it down and get word to us. Probably as bad as anything, lying out all night on the mountainside didn't help those two much."

I heard later that they both survived, though the one with the head injury had a rough time of it, being much worse off than had initially appeared. As Dick, who was the only one of us that had extensive experience with technical climbing, said, "That, of course, is the other side of the grandeur and isolation of the peaks. The mountain can hurt you, and she doesn't care one way or the other. You can be well-trained, well-equipped, and well-prepared; sometimes all that is just not enough, if your luck isn't with you."

The next week, up on the Hidden Falls Trail, things were com-mencing to smooth out. We still had plenty of rock work and blasting, but it began to go easier, and we began to be able to use our growing famil-iarity with the tools and the terrain to move more rapidly and with more assurance. As with all things, whatever fascination my near-death by shoot-ing at the hands of the Duke, and my daring escape by leaping from some un-named female's bed straight through a window (for that was the way the incident was generally portrayed) held for the crew was rapidly superseded by the succeeding waves of tall tales of other wild nights and willing women told on the part of others. Billy, who discounted very heavily, and very accurately, these serial exploits of his crew, just kept us at it, allowing the juicy gossip to grease our wheels of progress. Between the hard work, sunshine, Billy's songs, and the malarky, we were doing all right.

Jim proposed a super Sunday for the next weekend. He was going down on Sunday morning to where Petey lived with her grandfather, a few miles west of town, half-way to Wilson. He said they both would be delighted if I would come along, and we could see Petey's new mare. And for Sunday night, Jim and I had both been invited to have dinner with some of the older park employees, who worked on the road crew. I didn't know this interesting bunch very well, but Jim had more contact with them, since they all worked out of the motor pool, and spent their days on the roads within the park.

Petey's grand-dad had a log cabin up in the woods off the Wilson road. There was a small meadow behind the house, with a few corrals and out-buildings. In a corral was a young Paint mare, almost as pretty as Petey, not too big, about 12 hands high, and fiery and gentle all at the same time. We stood around and talked about the horse. It never ceased to amaze me how Jim and Petey would talk, literally, for hours on end about horses. Then Petey went into the corral and showed her off.

From my inexpert perspective, it was Petey who really got shown off. She would stand at the pony's side, facing to the rear. With a motion so smooth and rapid you could hardly see it happen, she would spring, or leap, or slide UP, onto the mare's back. The motion was so fluid you could not tell exactly what was happening, just that it had happened. Once up, there was no saddle, no bridle, no hackamore, nothing but the horse and Petey. They would go around the ring together, smooth as spring grass, Petey guiding the mare with only knee pressure, her hands held relaxed above her lap, or caressing the horse's ears and mane, whispering to her. She would speed her up, slow her down, turn her through figure eights. Bringing her to a stop, she would shift her right leg forward over the horse's shoulder to the left side, and slide off as seamlessly as she had gone on. Petey told Jim she was training the mare for barrel racing, so the two of them talked about that for another hour or so. Then Jim had a little trot around on the mare, looking like he knew what he was doing, but without Petey's absolute grace. Then, after I got some help, and a lot of laughter, getting up, I had my turn, *sans* grace and *sans* knowing what I was doing.

It was just one of those unforgettable days that stay with you always, a slow-moving day with lots of time to let slide by, in the heart of a beautiful country, some sandwiches and bakery doughnuts and lemonade, and the picture that lives forever of a glorious girl and a handsome horse.

In the light of late afternoon, Jim and I drove back into town, cleaned up at the garden hose, changed our shirts, and went on up to Moose, to Clyde's house.

Clyde Farrow was the road crew supervisor. A small and wiry man, probably in his late fifties, but looking much older, his situation was unusual for park summer employees in that his wife accompanied him to Moose each summer from their home in west Kansas. They lived in a small cabin in the park headquarters area where the year-round "permanent" staff had their lodging. Ida was a small, round-cheeked woman; she spoke very little, but still reminded everyone of their grandmother.

Clyde was another one who had survived the hard times of the

Depression, traveling the rails and finding whatever work he could, which was not often and not much. He had spent many years in the coal mines of Kansas and southern Colorado, and had two major souvenirs from work underground. One was a short and crooked left leg, where a collapsing mine timber in a cave-in had broken his hip. The other was a worn-out set of black lungs, which left him a whispery rasp of a voice, an accordion wheeze, and a consumptive cough. In defiance of both momentos, Clyde hopped in and out of his dump truck like a chipmunk, incessantly smoking Camels, hawking and spitting and hacking and gimping along, and always grinning like a demented gremlin. Never a rainy day for Clyde, and if it did rain, it made Ida's roses grow.

As Jim told it, Clyde was as full of tall tales as was Billy, but his were darker, much darker. They were stories of the labor wars and horrendous working conditions in the mines, the goon muscle in the migrant camps in California, hungry days and broken-down jalopies. The hard times he had lived through had not broken his spirit; most of the jokes he told, and he told many, were on himself. Ida would just keep smiling her apple-cheeked smile and look on the bright side of things. Clyde was as punctilious about his good grammar and soft polite speech as Billy Jiggs was about his bombastic profanity. He was never seen without his battered black Fedora, his bottle-thick eyeglasses, his faded bib overalls, and workboots encrusted with road tar and mud.

Jim said that every day the road crews would josh Clyde about what he had in his lunch pail, and if it was specially good or plentiful, infer scurrilously that it was Ida's reward for Clyde's fine loving the previous night. Clyde would just cough and hawk and spit and grin, but he never denied it.

That evening, over a good dinner, we heard stories aplenty of those Depression Dust Bowl days. William Ward was there at dinner as well, as was another old bird whose name I never caught, who never said a word all evening, just nodded his head in agreement at every recounted instance of how tough those times had been. Willam told us about the

Green River Ordinance, the town law adopted by other jurisdictions all over the country, that allowed anyone without "visible means of support" to be either escorted to the edge of town, or thrown in the local clink for thirty days. William had been arrested in Green River itself, the Wyoming town lying just a few miles west of Rock Springs along Route 30. He said it wasn't so bad: they only kept him in jail five days, and he was warm and fed for that time, and the only hassle was getting worked over just for the fun of it by the town cops when they brought him in, and having his stash of seven dollars taken from his wallet when they gave him his belongings back and tossed him over the town line.

Those old-timers are about all gone now, and all that most of us have with which to try to capture what they endured are Steinbeck's words, and Dorothea Lange's photographs. And, of course, the songs of Woody Guthrie and Cisco Huston, who perhaps sang it clearest of all. ©

The freight train I ride on, is a hundred coaches long.
You can hear the whistle blow for a hundred miles.
But if my train runs me right, I'll be home next Saturday night,
I'm nine hundred miles from my home.
And I hate to hear that lonesome whistle blow . . . .

~~~

I am a Dust Bowl refugee.
Just a Dust Bowl refugee.
From that Dust Bowl, to the Peach Bowl,
Now the peaches is killing me.

Yes we ramble and we roam.
And the highway that's our home.
It's a never ending highway,
For a Dust Bowl refugee.

I'm blowin' down this old dusty road,
Yes, I'm blowin' down this old dusty road.
I'm blowin' down this old dusty road, Lord, God,
And I ain't a-gonna be treated this-a-way.

Those old grizzled geezers like William and Clyde were still around, especially in odd corners of the West, in the late Fifties. I feel privileged to have had the chance to meet some of them, and to have heard the tales they had to tell. They had been, as Woody might have put it in a talking blues, "hung up, laid down, wrapped up, sold out, and just plain run over." Many of them, such as William, were never able to get what had been promising young lives back on track. Many of them found a transition back to stability through military service in World War Two. Many of them lived out their working lives, as did Clyde, with shovels and hammers, and dump trucks. And many of them finished up under the bridges. Just like Davy Jackson a hundred years earlier, Woody had it right, " . . . we come with the dust, and we go with the wind." ©

We were sitting with Petey in the bakery one evening early the next week, when she, somewhat hesitantly, brought up a subject that seemed to be bothering her: "You know, Jim, there are these guys around town, they call themselves the Black Hat Gang, for the obvious reason. They're just a bunch of four or five local kids, from in town here or the ranches around, but they like to put it on. Sometimes they come in here, try to get a rise out of me. They really don't cause big trouble in town, just drag their old cars, make a little noise, things like that. Well, the other night they were in here, and started talking about these two other guys from the Teton Park who had moved into town, and how they needed to be taught that Jackson was the Black Hats' place, and didn't have space or time for outsiders. I think they know about you and me, though they didn't say so directly, and I think they were sending you some kind of foolish message."

"Yeah, I've heard of those kids, " replied Jim, "and they are probably all juice and no spit. Don't worry about it, Petey, but let me know if they bother you."

Two nights later, Jim and I walked into the Horseman, and immediately noticed two things. The more interesting was a table at which sat three young, fresh-faced and very pretty tourist ladies, sipping a round of beers.

The other thing was the presence, at a table near the first, of three young men, already somewhat lubricated by the evening's refreshment. Two of them had their black high-crowned Resistol western hats laid on the table in front of them, and the third was still wearing his. They were engaged, as you might expect of any young men under the circumstances, in trying to encourage the young ladies at the adjoining table to take favorable notice of them.

The girls, for their part, feigned total unawareness of the looks, winks, and smiles coming from the nearby table, and affected not to hear at all the appreciative comments that the young men were making, ostensibly to one another.

In short, it looked like nothing was going anywhere, but neither was anything occurring that could be considered offensive to either group. Perhaps you could argue that the boys were somewhat amateurish, and the girls leading them on a bit, but that same scene was probably being played out in half the bars in America on that summer night in 1957.

However, Jim's professional pride was a different matter. "Watch me take that sweet candy from those black-hatted babies." He sat for a millisecond at our table, rose again, walked that cowboy walk of his over to the girls, removed his hat, smiled, said a few inaudible words, and that was all she wrote.

Jim and I spent an extremely pleasant evening talking and laughing and drinking beer with the three nursing students from Saint Paul, who had joined us at our table. They had come to see the West, and if Jim wasn't it, what was? The air was full of the promise of things to come, as we agreed to meet them again (and bring a friend) several nights hence at the small sort-of dude ranch over in Wilson where they were staying. They could have been triplets, with those open Minnesota smiling faces, that creamy skin, and that nursing student aura of experienced innocence.

The Black Hats, for their part, did not take kindly to being so completely aced-out. They drank more, scowled and muttered to each other, and cast the *really* bad eye repeatedly in our direction. After a time, the other two put on their hats as well, and they departed.

The evening was broken up when the girls' landlady/chaperone/rancher came into the Horseman to pick them up for the ride back to Wilson. She was slim, tanned, and tough-looking as a dog-chewed old boot. Invited to have a drink with us, Lacey ordered bourbon, neat, and tossed down the shot, delicately wiping her mouth with the back of her hand and long fingers. She had an admirably slim but curved figure, in jeans, high-heeled narrow-toed boots, and a buckskin jacket that had been around about as long as she had. Her short brown hair matched straight-at-you brown eyes, above a thin, but not humorless, mouth. She greeted me politely, but gave Jim a hard, long look (one of the few people I ever saw do that).

"Let's saddle up, girls," and with that she pushed back her chair, stood up and shook hands with me, two quick short shakes with a callused palm and a firm grip. I thought she was unbelievably sexy, even if she was pushing hard at the wrong side of forty.

After they left, there wasn't much more Jim and I thought we were going to do that evening, so we went out through the swinging doors onto the boardwalk, into the warm windless night, turning left to step down into the street that would take us home.

Spread in a rough arc across our path were the three Black Hats, the one in the middle slightly forward of the other two. He didn't say much, just spat at my feet and said, "Let's get going, and see what you've got. " He was about my size, maybe a little lighter, and he was wobbling ever so slightly. That looked good, because I was stone-cold sober. It was clear that we were not going to be able to walk around this one. Jim whispered behind me, "I've got your back. I'll watch the other two in case they get any ideas. Go to it."

I took the one step down into the dirt side-street. Responding to that instinctive telegraph, a small crowd had emerged from the Horse-man and elsewhere, and surrounded us, thus ensuring that what they wanted to see was indeed going to happen. I had a few seconds to think it through. I really had no hot desire to fight this guy, but he evidently did intend to fight me, and one determined side is all it takes. So we went to work.

He moved in at me, quickly but with a semi-stumble, and swung a long looping right hand that I could see coming all the way from Hoback Canyon. I had my right up, feinted with it, stepped in under his swing as close as I could get, and hit him a short hard left hook (my best shot, because I am left-handed) on the right-side angle of his jaw.

His black hat flew off, but he hit the ground before it did, and he stayed there for a few moments, on his hands and knees, shaking his head to clear it. At that tender age, I had not yet learned the golden rule which says that when you put your man down, the best thing to do is to move a couple of steps forward, and kick him, hard, in the chest several times. That is most likely to ensure that he will not make the mistake of getting up again, and thus minimizes the chances of somebody getting seriously hurt (including yourself). But I hadn't learned that yet, and so I took a step or two back, and waited to see what would happen. Sure enough, he got up.

He bent over, wobbling some, and picked up his hat from the dust. As he straightened, he skimmed the hat at me, and came in fast behind it, with that wild right hand again. The hat bounced off my left shoulder, I blocked his right with my left and his hat, and let him have a straight right hand on the nose. The punch traveled maybe eight inches, but he was coming directly into it, and you could hear the cartilage snap and crackle. The blood sprayed like tiny rubies in the yellow glow of the streetlights. The crowd, which had grown now, gave that excited grunt that means they are getting what they came to see, the bastards.

Black Hat grunted as well, swaying, and then sinking to his knees and then forward on his face, spreading what was left of his nose a little wider. I thought we had had just about enough, and I began to realize that he was drunker than I had thought. I could see him trying to struggle up again. I'll say this for him, he was game enough. I looked around at the crowd and said, "Tell him to quit, He's had enough. Let's end it." Nobody moved, nobody said anything, and nobody, not even his buddies, offered to help him.

So he got up once more, pretty slowly this time, and started to raise his hands. I didn't wait, just stepped in, hit him once with a left between his belly button and his breastbone, and then a straight short right to the heart. He folded like a paper sack, and that was that.

Jim kept his eyes on the other two, stepped forward, and picked up the hat, one hand on each side margin of the brim. Then he put his boot through the crown. He tossed the hat at the other two guys, and motioned for them to drag their partner out of there. I was just standing there, feeling the after-reaction, disgusted with myself, disgusted with the crowd, and disgusted with the whole deal. I hadn't wanted to hurt that kid, but I enjoyed winning a whole lot more than losing, and the entire shebang seemed pointless in its brutality.

Jim grabbed my shoulder. "Okay, slugger, you took care of him pretty good. Now let's get out of here." As from a great distance, I could hear the police siren coming towards us, and I let Jim lead me into an alley, across a few dark streets, through a fence and some backyards, and to our tent. As we moved down the alley, I thought I sensed, behind us, a shape in calf-high moccasins and buckskins. He was walking backwards, heel-toe, soundlessly, watching our backtrail. I imagined a skinning knife in his left hand, a trade axe in his right. He felt me looking, and turned his head. His grin was that of the wolf, or some other, more pitiless, predator.

I sat on the edge of my cot, my hands shaking hard enough that Jim lit two cigarettes and stuck one between my lips. My pulse was pounding with the adrenaline rush you only feel after the fight is over, and I was dizzy enough to lie back and watch the glow of the Coleman lantern spin on the tent canvas overhead. As I dozed off, I half-expected the entire police force of Jackson, cruiser lights flashing and guns drawn, to surround the tent and haul me off. But of course that didn't happen. I wondered what would play out when we met those kids the next time in town. But that didn't happen, either. We never saw those Black Hats again.

⏤ WYOMING, "LET 'ER BUCK!" ⏤

Monday morning, I had some sore knuckles, especially on the left hand, but otherwise no aches or pains. Jim and I had promised to go back over to Wilson that evening to visit the Minnesota nurses, and to bring a friend along to make a third. I couldn't think of anyone else to invite, and so up on the trail Monday I asked Rod if he wanted to come along to "meet some nice girls at a dude ranch over in Wilson." To my surprise, he readily agreed, and seemed pleased to be asked. Maybe it was the dude ranch rather than the girls, or maybe we had been underestimating Rod all summer, and all that he needed was a little nudge. Later in the day, all was revealed: "Steve, I'll go over to Wilson with you guys tonight, if one of these weeks you'll go over to Wilson rodeoing with me. How about it? I kind of get lonesome going over there alone all the time, especially when I come back knocked more than half silly by some mustang. I'll appreciate the company, and I bet you'll enjoy the sport." What could I say? I agreed, thinking that, since it was now well into August, perhaps the summer would draw to a close before I had to make good my end of the deal. Or maybe Rod would get kicked in the head by a bucking bronco and lose his memory. Or maybe I would go after all.

After work that day, Jim and I cleaned up in the Moose bunkhouse, sneaked a merely semi-gargantuan meal with the other guys (we weren't fooling Mrs. Green a bit, but she actually enjoyed feeding us on the cuff once in a while), and loaded ourselves into the Ford with Rod for the short trip over to Wilson.

The "L Bar L" (L-L) wasn't really much of a dude ranch. What it was, was a main house and a couple of rental cabins, with another place close by down the road where you could rent saddle horses. Behind the house and cabins was a set of wire enclosures bearing a sign, "Champion AKC Fox Terriers for Sale. Dogs Boarded." You could hear the little rascals yipping and whining (I never have been much for small dogs, thinking them mostly good for breakfast for large ones) as you turned in to the circular drive under the pines.

We were greeted at the door by the three Minnesota maidens, with Lacey standing behind them, and Linda, Lacey's partner, hovering well behind her. Linda looked to be about forty-five, a little worn around the edges, lumpy and frumpy, and rather annoyed at the intrusion. She rapidly disappeared, but kept popping in again from time to time, as if to make sure everything was on the up and up. Lacey looked to me just as she had in the Horseman several nights before: lean, clean, tough as beef jerky on the outside, but with a hint of softness underneath. Same boots, same jeans, a raspberry-on-white striped Western shirt with a yoke and pearl buttons on the front, pockets, and cuffs snug on her slight, wiry frame. She was silent, but cracked a half-smile as we entered.

The evening was sort of scrambled, at least to start off with. I think that, upon reflection, the nursing students, who were planning on leaving for Yellowstone very early the next morning, were not quite sure why they had invited us, and we, for our part, were not sure why we had come. Romance definitely did not seem to be in the air. Rod kept looking around him, as if he thought something might jump on him out of the shadows. Jim, for once, seemed to be off his feed, perhaps thinking of

Petey at the bakery, not ten miles away. But, as for me, I couldn't take my eyes off Lacey.

Perhaps as a fall-back to this awkward situation, or as a less-difficult alternative, everyone concentrated on getting drunk. The nurses got giggly, Jim got flamboyant, Rod got spaced-out, Lacey drank in a determined 'here's how to do it' sort of way, and I got more and more interested in where things might go with Lacey.

The final tableau I remember, before things took a decidedly different turn (for me at least), was an unusual one. Rod had his arms around all three of the nurses. He was somewhere out beyond Mars's orbit, with a glazed look, and appeared to be incapable of speech. Jim was staring morosely into inner, as opposed to Rod's outer, space, a posture I do not recall seeing him in before or since, and seemed to be decidedly confused. Linda, in somewhat the style of Lady MacBeth, passed silently, in ghostly fashion, through the room. Lacey got up and headed for the kitchen, and I fantasized (or was it fantasy?) that she gave me a glance over her shoulder. I rose to the occasion, in more than one sense, and followed.

Lacey was standing at the kitchen sink, with her back to me. I pressed the length of me against her, put my arms around her slender waist, gently cupped her small breasts, and kissed her left ear. She turned without moving away, crossed her arms behind my neck, one hand holding the half-empty bourbon bottle, and the other a jam-jar glass containing fresh ice-cubes. The long soft kiss she gave me started somewhere in Texas and ended on the northern Montana border. That was so good we did it again a half dozen times. If she had spilled any of that bourbon down between us, it wouldn't have had space enough to trickle on through.

I backed off just enough to start fumbling with the pearl snap buttons on her yoked western shirt. She stiffened, turned on her best killer frontier lady stare, and said, "Buster, if I got up around you, I'd probably break your back. I'm not sure either you or I are ready for this."

"Lacey, I bend but I don't break. And as for Ready, I'm already at Get Set, and Go."

She gave me a strange and, in retrospect, quizzical look, and replied, "Okay, cowboy, then I guess we better saddle up and ride." Lacey led me out the kitchen back door and into one of the small cabins. Drawing back the curtain to a side window to let the moonlight shine in, she lit a small bedside fuel oil lamp and, her eyes on me all the time, undressed herself and then undressed me. We lay side by side on the narrow metal cot; I watched the play of the silver light on her ribs and at the hollow of her throat.

Lacey's sexual energy had a yearning, questing quality to it that emptied itself only to fill up again and again. And I, of course, was nineteen. The long night's sensations expressed themselves to me, in a half-dreaming state, as visual images: a coyote, motionless and silent on the edge of a ridge, there, and then gone like smoke. A field of sunflowers, turning imperceptibly slowly, but inexorably, to keep pace with the energy of the light. A magenta dawn, spinning in speeded-up time to blazing overhead noon, and fading to purple and orange sunset. Cool water, running through rocky riffles, while the shadows of rainbow trout lay silent, downstream of the stones.

When I awoke, it was to the grey light of daybreak. Lacey was gone, the bed still warm and damp beside me. I dressed and went back through the kitchen door. Jim was sprawled, alone, on the living room couch, and opened one eye as I entered the room. "Good morning, Sunshine," he grunted. "Linda and Lacey have headed for Idaho Falls for supplies. The girls are on their way to Jellystone Park. Rod, so embarrassed he couldn't speak, hitch-hiked back to Moose before nine last night. That leaves just you and me and the Fox Terriers, pardner, and at least two of us need to be up at Moose in an hour or so. Better get a move on."

I hardly said a word to Jim all the way back to the park, my mind not quite in gear, off somewhere far away from the mix of bourbon, fatigue, and the lingering emotions and sensations of the night just past. Jim tried to start some schoolboy banter, but soon gave up the attempt.

"Jim, I've got to see Lacey again tonight. Will you drive me back over to Wilson after dinner?" He gave me an incredulous look, opened his mouth, shut it again, and just nodded his head.

By seven that evening, we were back at the L Bar L. Lacey's (or Linda's?) pickup truck was in the drive. Jim said he would wait in the Ford, and I knocked on the door. And knocked on the door. At the fourth try, the door opened halfway, and in it stood Linda, red-eyed and not at all pleased to see me.

"Well, what do *you* want?" No, Lacey's not here. Don't you get it, *boy*, she doesn't want to see you, not tonight, not tomorrow, and not ever. Beat it."

I stumbled back to the Ford, and just looked at Jim blankly, bewildered. Jim, older and more experienced, put it in simple English for me. "Steve, I thought you had the picture, but I guess you're dumber and greener even than I thought. Didn't you see what was clear from the beginning? Lacey and Linda are a *couple*.

———

By the middle of the week, up on the Hidden Falls Trail, we were leaving the rock face behind, and moving into shady forest, starting on the last of the trail sections, as we designated them, that paralleled the lakeshore and the old lower trail. After this section, all that remained was to swing inland and uphill across the rocky knob to reach the goal of two summers: Hidden Falls.

Cutting a trail is somewhat like a lot of parts of your life (including growing up): it's not exactly possible to say where one thing ends and another begins, they sort of flow into each other, intermingled. At some point, the head of the crew was, more or less, off the face and into the trees, while at the same time the tail of the crew was, more or less, still moving rocks around, and trundling up dirt to fill in between them. And there were some scattered big stones and boulders within the forest margin, outliers from an ancient rockslide. But there was a point when it became clear that we had left the one domain, and entered the other.

The nature of the work now changed markedly. Where there was dirt, shovels could skim and scrape and level. Where there were trees in the way, axes and cross-cut saws could trim them or cut them down. Stumps and roots called for pulaskis, axes, and shovels, and only occasional dynamite. The work was more refined, requiring greater parts of landscaping, and lesser parts of engineering, as compared to working on the rockface.

The comfort level increased as well. True, the weather was cooler now, in late August, especially in early morning and late afternoon. But the trees gave shade and drew breezes, and the soil was soft to sit on at breaks and lunch, and the dirt didn't sting your nose and throat like the sand and grit did.

We were leaned and oiled as a team now, and each of us knew better what we were doing. Billy could let up just a little bit on watching and criticizing our every move. He would even, for a few minutes, move up ahead and stand, hands on hips, looking up at the rocky knob, shaking his head to some private thought. "All right, you hapless hairy wollygollies, " he would say as he returned, "better enjoy this rest period while you have it, and save your zip for the last push, because she's a'coming for sure, and she's a'going to bust your tiny balls." But his heart didn't seem in it, not in the same way as it was before, and there was a gentler tone to his harangue, almost as if he regretted the coming end to the struggle.

The songs were sweet again, sweeter than any previously, but they also thrummed with the rhythm and percussion of hard work and good sweat. Axes and saws are nothing if not used rhythmically, in a way that shovels can never be.

So, as we began to believe that we might actually get her done before the season ended, and knew we had learned to hit harder but work easier and smoother, the best song for this period was, of course, the ballad of John Henry.

Everyone knows, or should, the story of the black man with the unquenchable soul, a man who actually lived, and worked as a track layer on a railroad tunnel in the mountains of Tennessee, in the second half of the nineteenth century. A man who not only knew how to measure twice and cut once, but also how to get it done, whatever it took. The steel-driving man whose muscle and bone would not yield to the machine, even to survive.

There are scores of verses to his song, and many versions, and Billy knew them all. Here are the ones that I think tell the heart of the story:

When John Henry was a little baby, sittin' on his mammy's knee,
He picked up a hammer and a piece of cold steel,
Said, 'This hammer's gonna be the death of me, Lord, Lord,
Hammer's gonna be the death of me.'

Well, the Captain said to John Henry, 'I'm gonna bring me a steam drill round.
I'm gonna bring me a steam drill out on the job,
Gonna whup that steel on down, Lord, Lord,
Whup that steel on down.'

John Henry said to his Captain, he said 'A man ain't nothin' but a man.
Before I let that steam drill beat me down,
I'll die with my hammer in my hand , Lord, Lord,
Die with this hammer in my hand.'

John Henry drove into the mountain, his hammer was striking fire,

John Henry drove his eleven feet of steel,
And the steam drill only drove nine, Lord, Lord,
Steam drill only drove nine.

John Henry said to his Captain, 'Lookee yonder what I see.
Steam done choke, drill done broke,
And it can't drive steel like me, Lord, Lord,
Can't drive steel like me.'

It was in these woods, in the final weeks of the season, that Billy really came in to his own, as a leader and as a teacher. He showed us things with the axe and the saw I would not have believed, if I hadn't seen Billy do them, and then tried, as best I could, to do them myself.

If you look up and down a tree, how she's made, and how she leans, and then cut your notch just right, and then chop from the other side, and work back and forth in good proportion— you can drop that tree just exactly where you want, right on the compass point. If your axe is sharp and clean, and your swing straight, you can work down the felled tree just like picking corn, lopping off limbs smooth and easy. If you keep your rhythm, and know how to let the axe head carry itself forward, you can work a long time, and not have to stop, rest, and lose your forward traction.

The bastard two-man cross-cut saw is another story. An axe will work with you; you have to match yourself, both of you as a team, to the rhythm of the cross-cut saw. Take a six-foot saw, maybe a little big for Teton trees, but still, all you have. Firstly, it's a bitch to carry up the trail, too short to fold over easily, and too long to comfortably carry as it is. The end handles don't keep you safe from the big saw teeth, so you run a good chance of snagging your shirt, or cutting your hand, as you heft and carry it. Secondly, two men have to work it, back and forth, and if you don't keep the flexible blade straight in the cut, if you get any angle at all from one side or the other, the blade will hang up and jerk on the blisters you get from pulling anyway. If you and your partner don't keep your stroke and rhythm even, the blade will hang up again, or, worse, try to jump out of the cut and take somebody's ear off. It takes a while to learn to not *push* the saw when it is going away from you, to only *pull* on it when it is coming back towards you. And you and your partner have to learn to coordinate it all, together: even rhythm, same length of stroke, the blade exactly in line up and down and side to side, start together and stop together, alternately pulling and then not pushing while the other guy pulls.

It's bad enough when you are cutting sideways, on your feet to cut through a standing tree, notched and marked by the axe to fall where you want it. But when you are sawing a big deadfall which is lying across the trail, and you are sitting down, feet braced out against the fallen trunk, sawdust flying in your sweat-streaked eyes, no good purchase for the pull: that's when the cross-cut will improve your vocabulary. And when, in either case, the tree sags into the running cut, and clamps down on the blade, so you have to drive a wedge or an axe blade into the cut to release the pressure and keep going, you will know why the best cross-cut saws are forged in Hell.

But when she is going smooth, and when your partner and you have it just right, and when you feel the sun on your back, through the top of the tree that you are cutting down, that flexible blade starts to actually sing, with a music no other tool can make.

And that is sweet music, indeed.

So we moved across that section like a hot knife through butter, our eyes ahead on the final rise across the rocky knob. And on one of those days, at lunch break, Billy moved over to the big tree against which I was sitting, offered me an apple, leaned back, and said, " I hear you have a way of getting yourself into trouble, Steve. That's not all bad of course, a kid your age ought to learn a little bit about trouble. Without seeing trouble you won't learn to appreciate the sweet side of life. And, Steve, you surely have a nose for trouble. Why, some years from now, when you're a big doctor and all, maybe you'll have a disagreement about a diagnosis or such with another specialist in the conference room. And then you can just knock him right on his ass, and that will be that."

"Well, thanks, Billy, but I'm not sure that's the way it's done."

"I know that's not the way it's done, you jerk-off bull's pizzle. That's the point that even a dim-wit like you should understand. You know, I give all the guys on the crew names, though I generally keep them to myself. Names that I think tell something about them, like the Nez Perce over in Idaho do. And the name I gave you is Stout-as-a Horse. And stout doesn't mean fat. So it's a good name. But if you eased back just a little, looked around a little more before you fired off your mouth, or your hands, or even your pecker, it would be an even better name. Might even mean reliable, as well as strong. Know what I mean?"

I thought hard about what he was saying, and, though I didn't like it, I could see the truth in it. And, as with most things Billy Jiggs said, I could tell that it would continue to ripen in me over time. "Thanks, Billy. And thanks for the apple."

— — —

On a Wednesday, almost mid-way through August, I had another phone message waiting from Kitty. I hadn't seen her since the Leigh Canyon fiasco, hadn't seen Dick either, as a matter of fact, and didn't know what had transpired regarding his absence from the trail camp, or how it had worked out between them.

"Steve, I had a message from Dick that he is coming out for the entire week-end, and wants to blow you and me to a steak dinner at the lodge on Saturday evening, to make up for what happened a couple of weeks ago. He also wrote that he has an idea he wants to talk with you about, but I don't know any more than that. Can you meet us at the rec hall about six?"

There wasn't much doubt about it. I would have, under any circumstances, gone anywhere from Hell to Breakfast to meet Kitty, and I was anxious to catch up with Dick and hear what he had in mind, so I sent a message back up, and it was arranged.

I spent Saturday trout fishing with Jim over in our secret lake up on the Continental Divide, and Jim dropped me off at the lodge on his way back to town with several hundred pounds of cut-throat (actually, we got skunked that day).

When I walked into the rec hall, where I had not been for several weeks, the first thing I saw was the Duke, reading a magazine, his lips moving, over in a corner. He looked up, and, not knowing anything better to do, I gave him a one-finger (index finger) salute, and turned it into a "bang, you're dead" pistol sign, with a wink. I think he tried to pretend he didn't recognize me, but a salmon-colored flush (I guess I was still thinking of all those cut-throat Jim and I hadn't caught) spread upwards from his collar to his big ears. And neither he, nor I, said a word.

Dick and Kitty were sitting over in another corner, close together on a couch. It was obvious that whatever differences they had thought they had, about the Lost Weekend, were far behind them. Kitty was flushed with a sort of an embarrassed rosy glow, and Dick looked a little vague and mumbly. I doubted that they had spent much of the Saturday trout fishing.

"Hi, Kitty. Hi, Dick. Kitty, have you put up any holiday boarders in the dorm lately? Dick, have you got your trained bear with you? It's great to see you, even if you do both look like your legs are too wobbly to hold you up."

"Okay, enough of that," said Kitty, one part embarrassed and one part feisty." I don't know how the devil that mess got started Monday morning. One of the girls I was bragging to in the wash room Sunday night about what an adventure we had had must have told somebody who told somebody. I'm really sorry you had all that trouble, but I'm glad it worked out alright. I told my boss here that, if they did do anything to you, I was quitting."

"Hey, buddy, the grapevine is all over the Tetons that you've been punching out all the bad guys in town. That bear is sure luckier than he knows that he left the camp before you got there. By the way, thanks for trying to clean up the mess, and for getting Kitty down." And that was all he ever said about it. I never did learn what had happened that day, and maybe Kitty didn't either. It didn't, somehow, seem important to talk about it further. If I had to guess, which I don't, it would be that Dick had seen the possibility of exploring a new stretch of mountain country, of looking over the next hill, and just plain *forgot* about Kitty coming up to see him, unlikely as that would seem to me.

"C'mon over here, Steve, I want to show you something." As Dick pulled out a quadrangle map of the Tetons, I moved over to the couch, and deliberately squeezed myself into the middle between my two friends.

"The end of the season is coming fast. Trail crew work closes the week-end just before Labor Day Monday. There is still a chance of mostly good weather up on the range, and I don't have to be back in Boulder for a week or two after that. Besides, Buddy has asked me to stay and help do a final sweep of the mountain trails and camps after we close down, just in case some greenhorn from Boston or somewhere has left an ankle up there.

"Now, I've got a friend among the horse wranglers at Jenny Lake, and they don't leave for Arizona until mid-September. So they've agreed to give us a couple of horses for four-five days, and my thought was that you and I could circumnavigate the range. Look here. We could ride down the east side of Jenny, down through Bradley and Taggert, all the way to Phelps Lake. Then we could head west up to the head of Death Canyon at Fox Creek Pass, then turn north through that beautiful high barren shelf on the western rim of the park, behind the peaks, all the way to Paintbrush Canyon and Lake Solitude. You could leave me at the Divide there, and bring both horses back out Paintbrush to Jenny. The exciting thing is that we would have circled the entire group of major peaks of the Teton Range, except for Moran, seen 'em all from the east, south, west, and north. Four days, maybe five. What do you say? Probably won't meet anybody at all along the trail, except maybe your old friend Jedediah."

"Dick. Let's do it. If it weren't for school, we could take in some snowshoes and stay all winter. Like those old guys. But, seriously, I'm in."

That set the mood for the evening, and we had a rollicking dinner, at Dick's considerable expense. We roasted that old bear from here to the Yukon, we dreamed about flying again over Yellowstone Falls, and we talked about all the wonderful things we had yet to do before the season was over, and we were bound away from the Tetons, back to our other worlds. But mostly, all I could think about were the Shining Mountains, having them all to ourselves.

———

On Monday, I had another invitation, this one not such an automatic, but enticing in its own way. It came in the form of a gentle reminder from Rod.

"Hey, Steve, there's only a couple of more weeks of Wednesday night rodeo over to Wilson. I'm going this week, could use the prize money and the exercise. I think it's about time for you to come along and get bronc-baptised. Ready?"

Wednesday after work, Jim, Rod, and I ate an early dinner at the bakery. Jim shook his head and said, "I can't believe this. I know you think you're Captain Marbles or Tom Mix or somebody, but you can barely stay up on Petey's young mare, let along anything that is determined to pitch you off. I was born on a ranch, been around horses, bad and good, all my life. Now I know I don't have much common sense, but I do have enough so that the last time I was on a saddle bronc was when I was in high school, and I aim to keep my record going. You, on the other hand, are just plain dumb as a bag of hammers, and are going to get nailed. I will ride you guys over there so I can see the fun and the disaster, but don't expect me to get your blood all over the Ford's upholstery bringing you back. You bleed, you walk."

Petey gave me a little peck on the cheek, and a squeeze around the ribs. "Don't listen to that wore-out poor excuse for a cowboy, Steve. He's just sorry for himself 'cause he thinks he's getting too old. Heck, I *know* he's getting too old, and losing his nerve, as well as his squeeze. You, on the other hand, are young and full of juice, and maybe old Jim better watch his sweetie around you, the John Wayne of Massachusetts. All the girls love a rodeo cowboy, and I'm no exception. Just 'let 'er buck!' "

"Thanks, Petey," I replied. "Maybe I would do better saving myself for you, but I guess I better go through with this, especially since my buddy here doesn't have what it takes any more to ride anything wilder than a garbage pick-up truck."

"I'll be pickin' *you* up out of that dusty arena, more than likely, speaking of garbage," Jim growled, unsuccessfully trying to suppress his grin.

"Okay, look, "said Rod. "This is all going to be fine. It's easy. All you have to do is stay aboard for ten short seconds, till the buzzer sounds. Then you slide off, or let the pickup riders haul you off, or get off any which way you can, maybe ask the horse politely to let you off. You can do it, and once you start, you'll never want to quit. And there's no way to quit, anyway, you either ride it out or get tossed over the moon. You can borrow my boots and my spurs, and even my big hat when you ride. When you come out of the chute, just remember to keep spurring, keep your free hand above your shoulders, and whoop and holler and think about blueberry pie."

This rowdiness went on for some time, and I know it was calculated by my so-called friends to make sure I couldn't back out. But I figured I could handle it. I had actually been to *see* the rodeo in Madison Square Garden, New York one time with my dad and brother, although that was a decade or so ago, but it ought to count for something in the category of experience.

As the Ford chugged over to Wilson, west of Jackson toward the Teton Pass and Idaho, I felt more and more, with each passing mile, like the hapless groom at a shotgun wedding: not sure about the whole deal, but keenly anticipating what was to come afterwards.

Wilson was, in those days, a little wide place in the road, full of not much. A few stores and bars, some houses clustered together and more scattered across the surrounding countryside, an area-wide school, and a sagging plank-board arena with some corrals, behind the school's baseball field. For the regular Wednesday night summer rodeo, there were several dozen cars and pick-ups and horse trailers parked by the arena, which was lit up in haphazard fashion for the event. Kids off the area ranches, and some cowboys from as 'far away' as Rexburg, Idaho (some forty miles or so) would gather on Wednesdays to put a few dollars in the pot, and see if they could take home a few more. But local rodeo in Wyoming was as much an institution as was high school football in Texas, and folks took it seriously, and knew all the local heroes.

They had bareback and saddle bronc riding, calf roping, and steer wrestling. They also had barrel racing for the cowgirls, and a trick roper-and-dogs act. That was it, with a five-dollar entry for each individual event, ten dollars for the roping and wrestling teams. Since there were only a half-dozen or so contestants entered in each event, it was winner take all (after arena expenses). You could win yourself perhaps twenty dollars (or more, since most riders entered several events), some bumps and bruises, sweet smiles from the Wilson girls, and your name in the Teton County weekly newspaper. Biggest Wyoming rodeo deal between Cody and Riverton.

The rodeo stock was borrowed from local ranches; the ropers, barrel racers, and steer-wrestlers, of course, brought their own mounts. There were hot dogs, beer, cotton candy, his 'n her outhouses, and a screechy-squealy public address system, managed by the usual laconic Western comedian announcer. I went over to the entry desk and laid down my five dollar entry fee for saddle broncs (Rod said it was softer on the tail-bone than bareback, and easier to stay on, too). The announcer (who was also ticket taker, event coordinator, and contest judge) gave me a strange look when I listed my hometown as "Boston, Massachusetts," especially since, at that point, I was still wearing my lace-up work boots.

This probably isn't the place to tell you about all the fine points of the sport of rodeo, and most of them I don't know anyway, but if you have never seen it, go find it. And go see it, not on TV, but at some local rodeo, big enough to draw the professional riders, but small enough to light up the hometown. You'll see what the spirit of the West is still all about.

I drew the slip with my horse's name, Sunfish, and that was not good news, since even I knew that a bucking horse who twists his belly up to the sky is said to be sunfishing.

Since there was no special area set aside for the contestants, Rod and I went over to a front row near the chutes, with Jim and Petey behind us, slapping us on the back. There was a crowd of about a hundred and fifty people, including tourists from Jackson, come to see the show. It was a good-natured, high-spirited Western crowd, and the announcer kept them stirred up with sarcastic repartee concerning the foibles of man and beast.

Saddle broncs were the first event of the evening, and I had drawn the fourth place of six contestants. Rod, who was entered both in saddle and bareback, drew the first slot. He came out of that chute, hard and fast but making it look easy, on a chestnut-colored horse improbably named April in Paris. He made a pretty good ride, sliding off behind one of the pickup men as the buzzer sounded, but he didn't take prize money that night.

The crowd gave him a polite hand, and he came over to me to switch boots, spurs, and hat. We watched the next two riders, neither of whom made it to the buzzer, and then walked over to what I had begun to think of as the Chute of Doom.

Sunfish was there waiting for me, and a couple of cowboys helped me up the slats of the box, and over onto the grey horse's back, between the narrow walls. He banged and kicked around a bit, making sure to slam my knees into the slats, just to let me know what was coming, and who was the top hand.

"Now, folks," drawled the announcer over the whine of the p.a system, "Old Sunfish is back tonight, and giving us the signal that he's ready, so let's give this next boy up a good hand. He's come all the way from Boston, Massachusetts, to show us how they do it back East, and to have Sunfish show him how we do it in Wild Wonderful Wyoming!" There was some hooting and stamping and a little bit of clapping. "This ain't no tea party, pardner" came from one wag up in the back of the stands.

"Nice horsie," I said, squeezed my butt down into the saddle, pulled down the brim of Rod's hat tight, held the reins in one hand as best I could, and nodded that I was ready.

The gate was swung open, the horse (and I) came out of the chute, and I think I remember what happened next. One second—one jump—me spurring and shouting. Two seconds, another jump with a little rump twist (his, not mine)—me no longer certain which way was north from up. Three seconds—Roll that Sunfish!—and I was airborne, up, up, and away.

Man, I didn't know anything short of Billy's TNT could throw my weight that far that fast. What goes up must come down, and I did, arms outstretched, nose plowing arena dirt and horse apples, knees bouncing me up in the air again, so I could experience a second landing on my face.

The lights flickered and steadied back on. I shook my head like a wet dog, felt around to see if any pieces had fallen off and needed to gathered up, didn't notice any blood or teeth in the dust. So I climbed back vertical, from hands and knees, to hands on knees, to upright, did my best to imitate Jim's walk, dusting off my jeans with Rod's dented hat, and waved, unsteadily, to the crowd.

"Well, let's give that Flyin' Tiger a hand, folks, he got sent about half-way home to Beantown on that one. You all come back and see

Sunfish toss another one next week, you hear? And our next rider, way over from the Lazy Double D ranch in Alpine, is . . . "

And that was the start and end of my rodeo riding career. Petey gave me a kiss, Jim gave me a soft punch in sore ribs, and Rod said, seriously, "You know, you could learn how to do that, if you keep trying." I said, hurting in places I didn't know I had, but learned to know that I had for the next week, "Thanks, Sunfish, let's do it again sometime."

— Up, up into the Shining Mountains —

Jim had to be leaving the park a week or so early to prepare for the opening of school over in DuBois, so on the Sunday following the 'great bronc-busting adventure and tenderfoot humiliation' (as Jim was fond of putting it), he and I closed out our place in Jackson. We had a farewell round at the Horseman, folded the tent and packed the gear, thanked Mr. MacGregor for the use of his garden, and left him a case of Coors. Petey helped us pack up, and after we tossed everything into the Ford, I held her close for a moment, and whispered to her, "Let 'er Buck, Shoshone maiden."

Jim and I replaced the camping gear in the storehouse at Moose, using the key Buddy had given us, but without making an undue fuss to alert anyone about it. Easy out, easy in, and nobody ever said anything to us, if indeed anyone ever had known about it.

Jim would return to Jackson, spend a day or so with Petey, and then head over to DuBois. Mrs. Green had agreed to re-install me in the bunkhouse, for seventeen dollars and fifty cents for the week that I would need bed and board, and so it was time to say goodbye.

"Okay, Jim, be careful with those DuBois honeys, especially if they're under sixteen. Maybe see you next summer."

"Yeah, Steve, maybe next summer. But I don't know, I'm thinking about heading north to Alaska, especially if it's Statehood Summer. Ought to be some wild times, lots of girls and almost twenty-four hours of daylight to look them over in. We'll see; I'd like to have a look around that big country up there."

"I know what you mean. Always something new to see. Travel well, Jim." And I watched the old black Ford with the bucking horse plates wheeze its way out of the park compound and turn south toward Jackson.

Back up on the Hidden Falls Trail, Cascade Creek lay just ahead of us in the forest, straightening for its final race down into Jenny Lake. The plan was to build the trail to, and from, the borders of the creek, well below the falls, and lay some rocks strategically within it to provide stepping stones. The creek was not wide enough to rate a bridge, and, besides, a good spring flood down Cascade Creek would take out any crude log bridge we could put in. So the hikers, and the horses, would have to get their tootsies wet on the Hidden Falls Trail.

"Now, boys," said Billy, "come along over here with me, and tell me what your crossed eyes and weak brains suggest to you." We could hear the whooshing of the falls up and around to our left, and see the rocky knob before us across the creek. "Now, have you learned something working with a master woodsman, I doubt that you have, but if you were in charge here, which you surely ain't, how would you lay the line from here on in, with the two objectives of coming right up on the falls, and getting across the stream to join the Cascade Canyon Trail?"

He wouldn't let us go over across the creek to reconnoiter, and we spent a few minutes articulating fruitless suggestions, or at least ones that were fruitless in Billy's eyes. If we turned left to the falls before crossing the creek, we'd be on the wrong side of the water at the falls. On the other hand, if we turned right, and went over or around the rocky knob, to back around towards the lake and join the main Jenny Lake Trail, we'd cross the creek, but be on the far side of the falls.

"You see, my dimwit boys, sometimes what is obvious is dumb wrong. We've been building us a single straight line trail, though it has plenty of bends in it, for almost two summers now. But now, by Hellfire, what we got to do is to add a curved T-head at the end of our trail. So, the left arm of the T-head goes, on this side of the creek, right up to the falls themselves. The right arm crosses the creek, connects back into the lower Jenny Lake Trail, and then you can proceed directly up Cascade Canyon, or, if you wish, continue around the west side of the Lake and circle back to the Jenny Lake Lodge."

Rod was thoughtful for a minute. "But Billy, if we just go up this side of the creek to the left, and also, on the right, cross the creek and swing around the rocky knob to cut back into the Jenny Trail, why then, we don't have to climb over the knob, blasting and digging rock, at all!"

"Well, Rodney, there might be some hope for you, after all, which is more than I can say for the rest of this sorry bugger lot."

"Wait a minute, Billy" I jumped in. "You must have known this all summer, probably last summer as well. All this bushwah about 'perspiration at Inspiration Point', and blasting our way every foot over the rocky knob, was just to keep us worried and going faster so we could finish up this summer."

"Well, ain't you the smart little bastard, Steve. You've got it, and for your heavy thinking, which must of wore you out, you get to carry the drill down tonight, and up tomorrow morning, though I doubt we will have much use of it from here on in. Boys, we are going to finish this mother bear this week, and beat the closing of the park work season, and be done with her!"

And from that point onwards, it was pure picnic. Up until now we had crossed the lake in the boat to the southern trail junction every day, walking the long way up the entire new trail to look for minor changes and improvements that could be made along the way, going over and over our handiwork with fine sandpaper. But from this last Tuesday on through the end of the week, we drove straight across Jenny Lake, to meet the old lower trail at the foot of Inspiration Point, one part of the crew working from there to cross Cascade Creek and connect with the head of the new Hidden Falls Trail, and the other part of the crew taking off from the Hidden Falls Trail junction to press along the south side of the creek, right up to the falls themselves.

And, truth to tell, we spent our rest breaks, and perhaps a little more time besides, jumping in the cold creek water, whooping and hollering and scooting around in the pools below the falls. And the biggest whale splash among us was made by Billy Jiggs.

What work there was went like lightning. We skimmed the soft forest floor, levered out a few rocks, had very few trees or big roots in our path. On Wednesday afternoon at lunch break, I asked Billy to come up the left-hand fork, the one to the falls, a hundred yards with me.

"Billy, squat down here low, and eyeball up the line. Tell me if you see what I see."

"By damn and horsefeathers, Steve, I think you might be right for once. There *is* a faint outline of an old trail here. Maybe that's partly why the going is so easy here. Makes sense, when you think about it. The animals, and the Indians, and maybe the Mountain Men as well, would have been going up to the pools at the base of the falls for hundreds, thousands, of years, maybe longer."

So it wasn't, in the end, a new trail at all, but rather a new cut at an old, old trail. Something about that felt good. And when, for the first time, we reached the base of the falls themselves, we found, lying on a flat rock, two tail feathers, magpie and Steller's jay. As if someone had left a sign for us.

We finished her up, except for the sandpaper, by Thursday noon. And as we sat, at the base of the falls, for lunch, Billy, for one final time, astonished us all. He reached into his left pocket, and pulled out his spectacles. Then he reached into his right pocket, and pulled out—a mouth organ. None of us had ever before seen him play the harmonica, and none of us knew why he needed to put his spectacles on to play it. But play it he did, and the music of the metal reeds rang round and round Hidden Falls. We were silent as he played all the songs we had sung together, and then played ones we had never heard before. And, finally, at the end, you could not be sure it was songs that he was playing, just wild, far, old, old music, from a creature of the woods and his pipes, wild music ringing off the rocky cliffs.

A trail, like the story of a life, is never really finished. There are places in it that change in perspective from year to year. Sections wash out, trees fall in the wind or from lightning strikes, rock roll down singly, or in slides. Every day, like a river, or like a life, the trail is a new trail, with new work to be done on it. And the day after we finished the Hidden Falls Trail, we could have started to build her again.

Friday afternoon (Billy kept us at it right up to quitting time), we were quiet as we rode across the lake for the last time. The park working season was ending that weekend, and most of the summer staff were taking off. I was to meet Dick on Saturday morning at the Jenny Lake Lodge corrals, to start our horse trip. Billy was headed home to Driggs, not to return until the next summer.

When we got to park headquarters, and jumped off the truck, and had stowed the work gear, I pulled Billy aside.

"Billy, I want to thank you, for all you've taught me this summer. It has been a privilege to . . . "

"Don't thank me, Horse. You done pretty good, and when you learn to use a little more head and a little less muscle, you'll probably do just fine. I hope I see you again, and if you ever need anything, you can always call Billy Jiggs. If you get over by Driggs, Idaho anytime at all, drop in and see me."

I did get over by Driggs, but not until thirty-four years later, and by then he was gone.

Saturday morning, as I hitched up to Jenny Lake Lodge from Moose, the sky was brilliant blue, with just the hint of an early morning bite in it, something I had not felt since late June. The peaks were sharply outlined, and the snow was at its lowest level of the year. The roadside meadows were more muted now, summer's riot of color fading fast.

Dick was waiting at the corrals. The young wrangler graciously introduced us to the two geldings he was lending to us. "This here is Blaze, and this other one here is Star. They ain't showy, but they'll get you wherever you are going. They speak pretty good dude, they don't spook easy, and they'd appreciate you carrying some oats for up high where the grazing won't no longer be good. "

There must be at least one Blaze or one Star in every Western horse string, and the Jenny Lake string had one of each. There wasn't a nickle's worth of difference between the shapes of the white splotches on their foreheads. Blaze was, all the rest of him, a sort of a dark Dr. Pepper color; Star was more a classic chestnut. They clearly were old buddies, and either gelding would follow the other, at a sedate and smooth pace, snuffling and farting softly back and forth from time to time, as if they were telling each other stories.

I tied on my gear behind Blazes's saddle, and Dick did the same on Star. We were traveling light: sleeping bags, two small tarps, as little food as we could get by with, ditto with the cooking gear, and a few other essentials. All our stuff rolled easily in the tarps. Spare clothing was mainly a poncho and an extra pair of socks. Our basic diet was going to be a trail mix of dried fruits, nuts, and chocolate, some tea bags and bullion cubes, and a good supply of elk jerky—all items in supply at the Moose Junction general store. I did see Dick sneak a can of peaches in his bedroll, and I had done the same with stewed tomatoes. Water would be no problem along the trail; in those days no one worried about contamination of water sources in the Tetons.

We rode out of the corral, and headed down the east side of Jenny, past the old boat dock and down the shoreline, the peaks shining in the morning sun across the lake. Just for the hell of it, we took the short detour around the Moose Ponds, and thus crossed the junction of the Jenny Lake and Hidden Fall Trails. The moose were not cooperating, or at least we didn't spot them, and we passed along to Lupine Meadows, faded and almost brown as September came on.

It was easy going, along the level forest trail, and as we looped by the mouth of Garnet Canyon, I remembered the spectacular vistas from a weekend campsite between Surprise and Ampitheatre Lakes, just a few miles up the canyon, looking up at the enormous walls formed by the heart of the range: Teewinot, Mount Owen, Teepee Pillar, Disappointment Peak, and behind, ever higher, the Grand and Middle Tetons. The two lakes lay at almost ten thousand feet, at timberline.

We ambled (for that was the single gait of Blaze and Star) down along the eastern shores of Bradley and Taggart Lakes. At the south end of Taggart, where we disdained the footbridge and splashed the horses across the shallows, Brother Moose at last made his appearance. Hearing the horses in the water, he raised his great head from the marshy weeds that he was feeding on, and turned it back and forth, slowly, to give us a respect-provoking view of his broad antlers. Snorting, he moved away, in that dainty and utterly graceful way that moose have of trotting through shallow water, fetlocks and hooves lifting rhythmically. Whoever falsely joined the images of moose and ungainliness had never seen them trot in water, nor run full tilt through woods, perfectly balanced, antler racks never touching branches.

It was a long and undramatic haul, better than five miles, from Taggart down to Phelps Lake, at the mouth of Death Canyon, where we would turn west to climb up into the mountains. After a short climb behind the lake, we stopped to rest the horses before heading into the canyon, looking down on Phelps and beyond to the Snake River and the Hole. Then, against all logic, we actually descended steeply to reach the canyon trail.

The first few miles of Death Canyon were hard going but spectacular, a narrow canyon with soaring walls, the roaring stream of spring and early summer now reduced to a somewhat quieter flow. The trail was narrow but, I noted, well maintained, and the steady grade was cut just the way Billy would have liked it.

Two or three miles into the canyon, the grade leveled out, the space widened, and we came to a patrol cabin, our first night's goal. Even though it was still mid-afternoon, we wanted to put a somewhat easier first day on the horses (and on our own rear ends). Besides, there was a trail crew mate of Dick's camped at the cabin, finishing up his summer's work, and we looked forward to an evening of tall tales and a good meal with him and his supplies. There was good graze here for Blaze and Star, and we passed a pleasant, if uneventful, night. We turned in early, because the next day was to be the longest, and most difficult, of the journey.

The morning of the second day saw us begin with a long, gradual ascent of almost six miles, up to the head of Death Canyon to Fox Creek Pass. At the top of the pass, you can see Forever: the flattened ridge of Death Canyon Shelf heading just east of north, Death Canyon itself back down the way we had come, and the slopes down to the green Idaho forests to the west and south. We rested man and horse a bit, and then struck out along the magnificent, barren, Death Canyon Shelf, running almost four miles.

As we moved out along the Shelf, we saw some more of Forever. "Hey, Steve, you see those two high peaks just to our left out in the distance? Those are Mount Jedediah Smith, and Mount Joe Meek, just waiting there for guys like you and me. Alongside Mount Meek is the pass, also named for Wild Joe, which will drop us into Alaska Basin."

I thought Jed's mountain was well placed for him. Right on the park boundary, hidden behind the main ramparts of the Tetons, and poised where you could trail off in any direction, but especially west to the Pacific.

When I told Dick that I thought Jed must have liked it here, he turned to me and said, quietly, "Well, Steve, I know you think that some-times you see those old guys, or feel their presence. I want to tell you that sometimes I see them, too. I don't know whether we see them, or sense the tracks they once made, or just what it is. But something of them is here, all right. I'll tell you though, better not make much noise about it, better not mention it to people. You might get yourself tossed in the looney bin, or I might get disqualified from flying. We'd better wait, until we are so old that people expect us to be foolish, or liars, or worse, before telling folks about it. Until you're fifty, or maybe even sixty. And they still won't believe you, even then."

Neither of us said much for the next hour or so, thinking about it. We crossed Mount Meeks Pass, and began the descent into Alaska Basin. We dropped down a final steep, rocky scree known as the Sheep Steps, where we had to go very carefully, and, once, lead the horses.

As we came to the first of the Basin Lakes, I headed Blaze over to a small copse of stunted spruce, to water him at the enclosed pond. With a sound like sharply tearing canvas, a huge Snowy Owl burst from the trees, straight over our heads, his wings pumping for altitude, with a span of well over four feet. He was there, and then he was gone.

Somehow, in a way that I never have been able to explain to my-self, it was all connected: where we were, how we were traveling, the conversation Dick and I had just had, the surreal burst of the white owl. I tied Blaze off to a tree, stripped out of my clothes, and plunged into the tiny lake.

"You're even crazier than I knew you were," Dick exclaimed. "Those lakes are glacier-fed, and today is September." But I knew, without know-ing why, that it was the right thing to do, and I think Dick knew it too.

The blooms had mostly gone from Alaska Basin, and we moved up the last mile or so to our destination of Sunset Lake. This would put us at the foot of the long, hard climb to Hurricane Pass, and we had decided to make that climb when fresh on the third morning.

We unloaded and staked out the horses, supplementing the poor graze with oats. Knowing the night would be cold, we set out our bedrolls in a way to guarantee warmth: find a pole that is long enough to reach between two trees, about three to four feet off the ground. Fasten one tarp to the pole, and weight the far end of the tarp with rocks, to make a low slanting shelter. Build a rock semicircle facing the shelter, and four or five feet from it, with the rocks piled high enough to reflect the heat of the fire into your cave. Build the fire small, using dry smokeless wood. Heads to the fire, sleep as well as you can anywhere on earth, with your bedrolls laid on the second tarp to keep the damp out. And, oh yes, if you can, position your camp so that you can look through the flames and see the Shining Mountains in the moonlight.

The climb up to Hurricane Pass is a hard one, and the pass well-named, because the wind blows hard and cold. A large glacier, School-room, is actually below you, and what is left of Forever that you couldn't see previously, you now see stretched before you. After a steep descent you reach the South Fork of the Cascade Canyon Trail, and easy going for the balance of the day. As we moved along, the peaks of the Teton core dropped astern, one by one. We stopped for a cold lunch at the junction with the main trail going down Cascade Canyon, and I thought of watching Dick head off from Jenny Lake, up Cascade, so long ago, on my first night in the Park. But, rather than turning down Cascade, we kept moving north, on the Lake Solitude Trail, toward our final camp, at the base of the Paintbrush Divide.

We dined supremely well at beautiful Solitude, on canned peaches, and canned tomatoes, and elk jerky. The cold lake water was sweeter than wine, and, brewed into tea, more soporific than chamomile. As the moon rose over Paintbrush Divide, I said, "Last camp, buddy," and Dick replied, "Last camp for *this* season."

The sunrise rays came early onto the top of the Divide, lighting fire to the reds, blues, and oranges of the Paintbrush Canyon clifftops. We did not wait for the light to ease on over to us where we were camped on the far side of the Divide, beside Lake Solitude. We rose in half-darkness, blew the campfire's embers into enough heat to brew a cup of tea by, and rolled up our gear. We didn't say much as we swallowed the tea and a bite of jerky, then saddled the horses and tied on the gear that I was taking back down with me. Dick stowed his few things in the soft haversack he was going to carry. I swung aboard Blaze, took the long hackamore lead rope that we had rigged on Star in my hand, and Dick and I locked eyes. He would hike back along the Lake Solitude Trail to the base camp down below the head of Cascade Canyon, and I would ride over the Divide and down Paintbrush Canyon to Jenny Lake Lodge, and away.

"Well, Dick, what a trip, huh?"

"Yeah, pardner, it's been a good summer. Maybe see you next summer, about the same time, and we can go fishin' again, eat pancakes, fly the mountains."

"Maybe next summer, Dick. Get all A's this year, especially in 'skiing and girls'."

"Will do. You know, if I get enough credits to graduate this year, I might be in the Air Force by next summer, flying for free. There's a lot to see in this world. How about that, maybe I could buzz you over the Yellowstone Falls."

I raised my hand, turned the horses, and began the long climb, two miles or better, to the top of the Divide above us, at ten and a half thousand feet or more. When, less than halfway to the crest, I turned in the saddle to look for him, he was already out of sight.

After switching back down from the top of the Divide, the trip down the canyon was easy and cool in the early morning, much of it in shadow. The creek was low and the land was dry, waiting for the snows of autumn and for next year's spring run-off. I took the longer way, just so I could pass by Holly Lake, and came out of the canyon mouth and into the forest between Leigh and String Lakes, turning south on the String Lake Trail for Jenny.

I was daydreaming in the saddle, thinking of that Sunday when Kitty and I had come this way together, when suddenly Star spooked mightily, rearing up against the lead rope. Lucky for me, I had a firm, if unconscious, grip on the line. A bear, a big one, came running full tilt, fast as his rear legs could drive him, making as fine a beeline as he could, from forty degrees to the rear on our left, and across our line of travel, about fifty feet ahead of us. Like an arrow, and silently, he flashed by us, and then disappeared into the trees.

I got the horses calmed down, and tried to figure out what could have happened to make a bear take off that way. The only thing I could think of was the jangle of a set of riders surprising him on the backtrail, but there were no riders behind me up here this day. And the bear had come from behind me.

Before nine in the morning, I reached an aspen-bordered glade, and decided to rest a while; I had a long set of days ahead of me. And, in truth, I wasn't quite ready to end the horse trip, nor leave the mountains, just yet. I unpacked and hobbled Blaze and Star, and staked them on long lines for good measure, just in case that bear might still be around. I leaned myself back against a tree, the sun warm on my face. The breeze was soft in the aspens, and I closed my eyes.

I felt myself awakened by the soft nudge of a moccasin toe against my leg. Raising my arm to my forehead, to shield my eyes from the glittering diamonds of the sun, I could just make out two horses, blanket-saddled, and two mules, heavily packed, grazing on the other side of the clearing with Blaze and Star. Above me towered two figures, ill-defined in the dancing sunlight.

"Hey, Old Son, don't sleep the best part of the day away. In the old times up here, you could lose your hair doin' that. Me and Davy will set with you a while, afore we have to move on. We're headin' up for the Bitterroots, and need to get there well ahead of Old Man North Wind. There's still grizz up there, and I want to see 'em. Then we'll turn a bit east, and winter with the Crow people, be warm in their lodges 'till spring. But Davy has been after me to go the other way this year, south-east across the Wind Rivers, where the Shoshone are now; he's sweet on a little Shoshone gal, and would like to spend the winter there. So maybe we'll go one way, and maybe we'll go t'other, and whichever we don't do, we might do next year. We'll see. You could ride with us, boy."

And Jedediah Smith hunkered down on his heels next to me. Davy Jackson, who had yet to speak, put his back against an aspen, his eyes always on the alert, scanning for any sign of trouble, with his long rifle across his knees.

And I could see, with a flash of recognition, that Jed had Dick's round face and easy manner, and that Davy had Jim's pale ice blue eyes, and self-contained kinetic energy.

"Jed. Davy. I didn't hear you come up on me. I must have dozed off."

"Well, wasn't it that feller who said we come with the dust and we go with the wind?" said Davy. "How about it, Horse, you a'comin' with us?"

"Jed, Davy, I, um, I, yes, I want to, but, no . . . I can't. Not this time. Maybe next summer."

"Well, boy," replied Jed, "we'll be at Rendezvous in early July, over on the Green River. There are just a few of us every year now, but you'd be welcome."

I thought of my good-byes and half-promises to Jim and Dick. "Yes, maybe next summer. Rendezvous. Down on the Green, beyond Union Pass, south of here, early July."

"You know," persisted Jed, "there's wonderful things awaitin' in these Shinin' Mountains. There's the Montana grizz, and in a few weeks, when the snow geese come down from the far north, in their tens of ten-thousands, you can hear their wings like thunder when they rise up from a lake at dawn. And, later, when the tundra swans come down along the big rivers, in their thousands, they follow along the bends of the rivers, so that the course of the river is mirrored in the sky, milky white. And further north yet, way up to Alyeska, I heer'd that when the salmon run in the summer, there are so many that you believe that you could walk across the rivers on their backs. And there are places up there where the big bad Alyeskan brown bears, bigger and badder than grizz, even, they come down to the rivers to feed on the salmon, scores of bears gathered together. They jump in the water on those salmon, or they stand at the tops of the little falls, and catch the leaping fish in their jaws. And they are so busy with the salmon you can fish right alongside of 'em, you and them bad bears together, and they'll pay you no mind. And the eagles come to you on the sandbars, and take the bears' leavings. I'd like to get up there and see that, one of these years."

"Jed, I will see that too, someday, and maybe we can see it together."

"And what about down south?" put in Davy. "Beyond the Shoshone, way down toward Santy Fee, there are aspen groves that cover a whole mountainside, and you can ride for a full day, and not see the end of 'em. And, besides, there are them pretty senoritas. And, way further south, in Mexico, there is a mountain valley where all the butterflies in the world come to winter, and they carpet the grass like a blanket of black and orange snow. I got it from a trapper, who was told so by a Indian."

Jed leaned close, gave me a slow wink, and whispered, "Listen. The beaver is comin' back, boy. Not a lot yet, not like before, but they is comin' back. And maybe even the buffler is comin', too, and if the buffler come, the free Red Men will come. And if they all come, then the Mountain Men will come, and won't we have Shinin' Times again! You ought to be here to see it, boy. Johnny Colter is always sayin' that there's things all along these mountains, from end to end, and side to side, that no one can believe until you see them for yourself, and he's right."

My eyes were heavy with sleep, and hot with tears. " I will, Jed, I will keep coming back, just like you did from Missouri. These mountains will stay with me."

"Well, then, like you say, maybe next summer, Horse."

When I awoke, I was alone in the silent forest, not even a jay crying a warning in the trees. The sun, high now, had dried the grass, so there was no sign I could read of men or stock having been in the glade, maybe just a few bent-over stems here and there.

It was only a few miles further to the Jenny Lake corrals. I made short work of hanging up the tack, turning out the horses, and thanking the wranglers. One of the boys gave me a lift down to Moose.

I went to the empty bunkhouse, showered, and collected my gear, already packed in the Gladstone. I hunted up Mrs. Green and Corey, and gave the former a hug (she blushed clean up to the roots of her wig) and the latter a salute. Corey instructed me for the fiftieth time as to where the best place was to stand for a hitch south out of Jackson for Hoback, and Mrs. Green insisted in finding me 'a little snack' to stick in my bag.

No one else was around, and so I crossed the headquarters yard for a final time, out to the park road, headed south. The light was fading, and the mountains were backlit with shafts of a fierce pink glow—one last song to my heart. Above the valley flats to the east, I thought I could just pick out Vega emerging in the darkening sky, only twenty-three light-years away.

I placed my Gladstone on the ground between my legs, faced myself north to catch any oncoming cars, and raised my right thumb. In my left hand, I held up the hand-lettered sign, black crayon on cardboard:

MOOSE, WYOMING TO BOSTON— OR BUST!

~ BUILDING TRAIL ~

I continued to carve out the trail of my own life, of course, yard by yard and year by year.

As time went on, I developed other friends, but none held so dear in my heart as Dick and Jim, though our time together had been brief. I had many teachers, but none who deserved more respect than Billy. And I had many mentors and exemplars, but none who were more substantive in their influence than Jedediah and Davy.

I became a physician, a pediatrician, and loved the relationship with my patients and their families, and the physical, intellectual, and spiritual challenges of doing my best, and being my best, in the daily struggle. But the Summer of Fifty-Seven had opened my eyes to the possibilities of cutting your own trail, and not necessarily following one already made. It was clear to me that I did not want, and would not flourish within, the confines of a middle-class American suburban practice, though my own roots lay within that context.

John Kennedy and the Peace Corps offered me another track to lay my line of trail along, and I spent two years as a young physician in the high Himalayas of Nepal. That, in turn, opened my eyes to the wider horizons of public health, and I gradually built my way, not without significant discomfort and ambivalence, away from clinical medicine and towards that broader domain. And that, in turn, led me overseas again, this time to the deep heart of Africa, and, later, to the still-wild North of Canada. But those are stories for another day.

Most of my professional life has been spent in public service, or, perhaps more honestly, in the search for adventure in the guise of public service. I rose to positions of responsibility, had my several five-minutes of fame or notoriety, most often based on conflict. I have never fully mastered "measuring twice so you can cut once"; judicious discretion has not been my strong suit, and I hope that would not be too much a disappointment to Billy, who himself loved to whoop and holler. In the end, I realize that nothing surpasses, for me, the experience of being a lone doctor in the bush, in the wild places of the world, doing what you can with what you have.

I lived through marriages, divorces, pairings, partings, children, and the sunrise of grandchildren. I learned that most of the pain and ill-fortune I encountered was brought by me upon myself, and that most of the joy and good-fortune that came my way was bestowed upon me by others. That lesson, of course, began in the Shining Mountains.

During the years, I returned as often as I could to the Tetons, sometimes just passing through, sometimes entering within them again. There are many seminal events and passages in most lives. Some of them come before we reach an age of consciousness, some come too late to significantly alter the direction and the lie of the future trail. But some come at a point, whether on rockface or in forest, where all further trajectory is reshaped and new directions set. I knew that that Teton summer was one such, perhaps the major one, for me. And so I kept coming back, as I had promised Jedediah, with a sense of renewal as well as contemplation.

As I matured, I often asked myself the question that, to me, contains one of the primary mysteries. Did those mountains really change me, actually open to me a new life? Or were they, rather, only the Shining Mirrors that reflected upon me what was already there within me, inevitably set in place, waiting only the opportunity for release and unfolding. In the end, perhaps, it does not matter much, but I would like to know.

Whatever the answer, the wild places of the natural world held, and still keep, the contexts in which I am most alive. I followed through on my other promises to Jedediah. I have seen the riverbridge of salmon, the sky full of wings, the giant ferocious bears, the plummeting mating flight of eagles, the mountainsides of autumn-flaming aspen. And, as Johnny Colter said, I now believe that these things are so. I have not yet seen the Valley of the Butterflies, and many other wonders that lie out there, and so there is much still to do. The most precious core, for me, remains that great chain of Shining Mountains, stretching from Alaska to Mexico. I now live at a canyon's mouth near their southern end, and thus can walk within them whenever I please, and feel at last that I have come home.

I recently was in Jackson Hole again, just passing through, coming down from Montana and the Yellowstone. It was autumn, past the peak of color, but still the world was at a height of beauty. The sedges and grasses were russet, the oaks, cottonwoods, and aspens orange and gold, the spruce and pine dark green. Intermittent spitting snow vied with blue sky sunshine.

A new highway had been built through the Hole since I had last come this way; I was momentarily disoriented to find myself approaching Jackson Lake on the wrong, or uphill, side of the lodge. A sign posted at the takeoff of the old road down to Moose via Jenny Lake said, "Avoid road construction delays. Take the detour."

For me, of course, it was no detour, but a central line of the spirit. I was alone, but not really alone. With me was a good dog, companion of a dozen years. We are both grizzled and grey at the muzzle now, and stiff in the joints after any modest day in the field. We rolled down the "detour" and pulled off at the first turnout for a head-on view of Mount Moran. There she was, bulwarked against a cloudy sky, girt with glaciers and crags. South of her were the deep canyons and soaring peaks of the heart of the Tetons.

We took the loop road along the east shore of Jenny. The lodge was closed for the season, but a few tourists were at the lake turn-outs, cameras clicking. The Lupine Meadows were brown.

I found, with some difficulty, the old park headquarters above Moose. The sheds and workshops were now clearly for secondary use, but the old bunkhouse/dining hall stood, apparently deserted, in a cluster of aspens that I remembered as saplings. A clutter of staff houses showed where Jim and I had Sunday dinner with Clyde and Ida, near a half-century earlier.

We rejoined the "new" road, which bypassed the Chapel of the Transfiguration and the old pioneer ferry across the Snake. I turned onto the side road for the chapel, which stood open but silent and empty at that weekday hour. Entering, I sat quietly for some minutes, giving thanks for the good things that had come to me, and asking for the grace of protection to come to all those who were on the mountain, or in harm's way.

A "new" park headquarters and visitor center lay along the main road through the Hole, backed by "new" staff housing that included a multi-story dormitory or apartments. Inside the visitor center, my vanity prompted me to engage the young summer park ranger on duty in discussion about the Hidden Falls Trail. He appeared rather bored with my old man's reminiscence, but I noticed that a second youngster, down the counter a ways, was hanging on every word, and that he had that look, Dick or Jedediah's look, in his eye. So it goes on, and hopefully always will.

But it was clear that the park had changed, its facilities modernized beyond the technological conceptions of Fifty-Seven. And its crowds of visitors are far greater than anything we might have imagined then. I had written the park superintendent a letter some months earlier, explaining that I was working on the book you are now reading. His courteous reply included the following: "Thank you for your letter about visiting Hidden

Falls. As you probably know, the Hidden Falls area is the most heavily used spot in the park's backcountry. Your trail work is used by over a thousand people per day during the busy part of the summer . . . The only old-timer that is still around is D—L—. He came to Jenny Lake in about 1960, so you may have crossed paths. D— is a volunteer in the park, and is working in the auto shop most days . . . ."

I drove down into Jackson. The town has mushroomed to near-unrecognizability, given the mixed blessings of a major ski area and four-season tourism. In some ways, it looked like a cross between Aspen and Atlantic City, but traces of the magic are still there. The modest commercial acreage I remembered has now grown many-fold, fronted with trendy Western shops, T-shirt outlets, up-scale art galleries, and restaurants. The Silver Dollar is still there, but its restaurant area has a slight aura of fern bar. The Horseman is gone, and in its place is a glitzy clothing and knick-knack emporium that does a thriving mail-order catalogue business. No-one I queried could remember the old bakery, and I could not find Mr. MacGregor's garden.

I checked into one of the score or more of motels, and ate a "New York Steak" at New York prices in a restaurant that was endeavoring, not entirely successfully, to be more Continental than Cowboy. Sleeping poorly, my dog and I were up at four a.m, and made a quick tour of all-paved streets before departing in the dark for the Hoback Canyon and Route 191.

Houses, street lights, gas stations, and schoolbus stops extended south from town well into the mouth of the Hoback itself, and I was glad, in a way, that I could not spot the old line-shack as we moved south, if indeed Cowboy Heaven still exists.

Full daylight came upon me as we slid down the long hill to Rock Springs. I felt the emotion that has been perhaps the most common of my life: a strange and incongruous combination of unsatisfied restlessness and deep contentment.

And then the sun came up, and I realized that I was in autumn's light in Wild Wonderful Wyoming, headed south for home—one mountain range behind me, and another before, yet to be traversed, and joy rose in my heart.

~ Epilogue ~

Many years have passed, almost a half-century.

Some of this is conjecture; some I know. Some is as True as only Make-Believe can be.

Billy lived well into his seventies, hale and hearty to the end. He died where he was born, in Driggs, Idaho, surrounded by his ten grand-children and their parents. Billy is up there on Heaven's Mountain, get-ting everybody organized, still laying out trails to beautiful places, show-ing newly-arrived greenhorns how to do it right, how to measure twice so you can cut once.

I never saw Jim again. When I lived briefly in Wyoming in the 1970s, I looked all over the state directories, but couldn't find his name. I tried the same with Nebraska, but no luck. Wherever the turbulent decades that came after the Fifties took Jim, I'm sure he eased his way along, looking fast but moving slow, with that cowboy smile and gift of gab. My guess is he did not end up with Petey.

Dick and I wrote a few letters, but neither one of us was much of a correspondent. He did, as I said earlier, fly a career with the Strategic Air Command, and then he flew commercial for some years. Last heard of, in the Eighties, he was living in Steamboat Springs, still in the mountains, and still on the ski patrol. I traced him there, and we exchanged letters and photographs. We were both over-the-hill guys running marathons on busted-up knees. Studying his bearded photo, I was surprised at how much alike we had grown to look.

Way back, in the autumn of 1957, I thought about calling up Kitty, who was at college only ten miles from me, and asking her out. But then I realized that there was too much of Dick Robbins, and always would be, between us, and I let it go.

Jedediah and Davy are still up there somewhere, as are all the old Mountain Men. If you stand in a breezy grove of aspen anywhere in the Rockies, you can sometimes hear the creak of their saddle leather as they trail along, endlessly on their way. If you get up real high, above timber-line, once in a while, out of the corner of your eye, you'll catch a flash of sunlight glinting off of metal far below—a rifle, an axe, a beaver trap—and you will know that they are there. May their spirits ride forever.

The Shining Mountains endure, themselves unchanged, though much has changed around them.

As for the Hidden Falls Trail, it's there, you can walk or ride it. If you go all the way to the end, up to Hidden Falls, and stand in close under the water's shimmering music, you might hear Billy's song. Yes, the trail is still there; we built it to last.

Stephen **C**. **J**oseph began his life in medicine as Peace Corps Physician in Nepal. Later, he spent three years in Central Africa with a team establishing a new medical school. He has been Chief of Pediatrics in a remote northern Canadian health zone, and a senior professional with both UNICEF and the Agency for International Development.

Dr. Joseph was also Commissioner of Health of the City of New York (his book on the early years of the AIDS epidemic, "Dragon Within the Gates," was published by Carroll and Graf), Dean of the University of Minnesota School of Public Health, and Assistant Secretary of Defense for Health Affairs. He is an elected member of the National Academy of Science's Institute of Medicine, and a former Executive Board Chair of the American Public Health Association.

An avid outdoorsman (though born in Brooklyn), Dr. Joseph resides in Santa Fe, New Mexico with his wife, Elizabeth Preble, and their dogs and llamas.

www.ingramcontent.com/pod-product-compliance
Lightning Source LLC
Chambersburg PA
CBHW011739010726
47496CB00010B/2998